A

Janine

A SENSE OF WONDER

Edited with an Introduction by
Sam Moskowitz

NEW ENGLISH LIBRARY

All of the characters in this book are fictitious,
and any resemblance to actual persons, living or dead,
is purely coincidental.

Originally published 1967 by Doubleday & Co. Inc. in the United States of America
under the title 'Three Stories'.
First published in Great Britain by Sidgwick & Jackson Ltd., in 1967
This edition © by Sidgwick & Jackson Ltd., 1967

'Exiles on Asperus'. Copyright 1933 by Gernsback Publications, Inc. Reprinted
by permission of the author and the author's agent, The Scott Meredith
Literary Agency, Inc. 'The Mole Pirate'. Copyright 1934 by Street & Smith
Publications, Inc. Reprinted by permission of the author. 'The Moon Era'.
Copyright 1931 by Gernsback Publications, Inc. Reprinted by permission of the
author and the author's agent, The Scott Meredith Literary Agency, Inc.

First NEL Edition February 1969
New edition, December 1974
Reprinted August 1977
Reprinted August 1982

NEL Books are published by
New English Library, Mill Road, Dunton Green, Sevenoaks, Kent.
Editorial office: 47 Bedford Square, London WC1B 3DP
Made and printed in Great Britain by Hunt Barnard Printing Ltd., Aylesbury,
Bucks.

British Library Cataloguing in Publication Data

[Three stories]. A Sense of wonder.
1. Science fiction, English
I. A sense of wonder   II. Moskowitz, Sam
823'.0876'08[FS]   PR1309.S3

ISBN 0-450-02247-1

CONTENTS

Introduction

SAM MOSKOWITZ

*Wonder is the opposite of cynicism and boredom; it indi-
cates that a person has a heightened aliveness, is interested,
expectant, responsive. It is essentially an 'opening' attitude
. . . an awareness that there is more to life than one has
fathomed, an experience of new vistas of life to be explored
as well as new profundities to be plumbed.*

Rollo May, MAN'S SEARCH FOR HIMSELF

There is one thing that all of the three short novels in this
book have in common. That identifying quality may best be
termed 'a sense of wonder'. They impart to the reader an
emotional breathlessness as well as intellectual stimulation. A
major failing of too much recent science fiction is that it
conveys no such literary 'magic'. It seeks to make the most
profound and thrilling mysteries commonplace. It substitutes
the shrug for the gasp. Before the term science fiction was
coined, the label 'scientific romance' was popular. Too often
modern science fiction has dispensed with the romance.

The three stories here are written by authors who are
ranked among the leaders in *modern* science fiction. Yet they
are veterans in the field: Murray Leinster appearing con-
sistently since 1919; Jack Williamson since 1929; and John
Wyndham since 1930. They were pioneers in certain of the
elements that are best in modern science fiction: superior
characterization, smoother writing, stress on psychological as
well as physical factors, and an air of sophisticated maturity.

'The Moon Era' by Jack Williamson appeared in *Wonder
Stories*, February 1932; 'Exiles on Asperus' was published
under John Wyndham's actual name, John Beynon Harris, in
Wonder Stories Quarterly, Winter, 1933; and Murray Leinster's
'The Mole Pirate' was the cover feature of *Astounding Stories*

for November 1935. Despite their early date of publication, the reader will find all the elements of modern science fiction in them, far in advance of the later trend, and they will also be found to be saturated with 'a sense of wonder'.

Murray Leinster (pen name of William Fitzgerald Jenkins) was nurtured by Robert Davis, famed editor of the American *Argosy*. His first true science fiction tale was 'The Runaway Skyscraper' (*Argosy*, February 22, 1919), where the Metropolitan Life Insurance Building of New York (then the world's largest) and all of its occupants are carried back in time to the period before the Dutch settled in Manhattan. This was well received, but not nearly as enthusiastically as 'The Mad Planet' (*Argosy*, June 12, 1920), a story which starts in a nightmare world, where all insects and plants have become so immense that man is but a mite who has reverted to loincloth and spear in nature's savage new plan.

Leinster later utilized his predilection for the writing of science fiction to plot a different type of mystery story for *Detective Fiction Weekly*, a companion to *Argosy*. The story, 'Darkness on Fifth Avenue', tells of a criminal genius who invents a device for casting specific areas of New York into utter darkness, even in the middle of the day. The story was shunted back to *Argosy*, where it was featured in the November 30, 1929, issue.

'The Mole Pirate', included in this volume, combines the finest elements of two facets of Leinster's writing. Like 'The Mad Planet', it involves utterly unique adventure and exploration, in a zone infrequently handled in science fiction, the actual body of the earth itself. Like 'Darkness on Fifth Avenue', it is a story of crime and mystery, with a master criminal to be tracked down and stopped.

Stylistically, 'The Moon Era' by Jack Williamson is modelled after the manner of A. Merritt, the famed author of 'The Moon Pool' and 'The Dwellers in the Mirage', but the plot treatment comes out of 'The World Below', by skilled British writer S. Fowler Wright (better known to mystery story fans as Sidney Fowler). In Wright's novel, our man from the present disembarking from his time machine, saves a female-like creature from death at the tentacles of a flesh-eating plant. In the evolutionary scale this creature is so far above him that he reasons: 'I thought that she regarded me much as we should do a half-tamed dog, ferocious, but

8

amenable to kindness and reason, and of a possible loyalty.'

A very similar situation is taken by Jack Williamson and in 'The Moon Era' developed into a relationship between alien and human in mutual peril of such delicacy and feeling that the story becomes a complete success in the tradition of A. Merrit, conveying the elements of constantly new mystery and wonder, in addition to a mood of tender hopelessness.

The contribution of the internationally acclaimed British author John Wyndham to this book, 'Exiles on Asperus', is in certain respects a landmark in the history of science fiction since it is one of the earliest important stories to successfully add to the basic elements that contribute to a sense of wonder the modern findings of psychological science. A very substantial share of science fiction since World War II has been weighted on the psychological reactions of humans and aliens to the marvels of future science and exploration, rather than on the marvels themselves. Indeed, in scores of stories, this phase of science fiction's development has been carried far beyond the psychological into the psychiatric.

The purpose of this volume has been to display both by word and example what the editor means when he uses the term 'sense of wonder' in relationship to science fiction. In the process, three truly marvellous short novels have been rescued from pulp oblivion. This is the first time any of the stories in this book, despite the fame of their authors – Murray Leinster, Jack Williamson, and John Wyndham – have every been reprinted since their initial publication. Beyond the considerable entertainment quotient of these stories, it is hoped that their examples may make a significant enough impression so as to bring about not a substitution of this type of story for what is written today, but an *incorporation* of the elements they contain into the mainstream body of modern science fiction.

Exiles on Asperus
JOHN WYNDHAM

FOREWORD

Whatever our private opinions – and they may differ a great deal – of the administration of Earth's colonies in the Solar System, we are, nevertheless, proud of their existence. Not only do we admire the men who founded them, but we are even prouder of the endurance of danger, hardship and discomfort by those who developed them. Few of us would care to spend even a week at a trading station upon Venus, yet many a man has worked for years in that eternal blanket of steamy mist, helping to increase Earth's comfort and wealth.

Not many of us would endure without protest a term of scorching by day and freezing by night upon the desert plains of Mars – that greatest of our colonies, so woefully mismanaged until the revolt of 2077, as to be like a stinging slap in the face of Justice. And still greater would be our trials if we should be forced to fight against the gravitation of the major planets.

Earth has cause, indeed, to be proud of all her colonies – all, that is, save one. The name of this one colony will be found in no directory; it is officially unrecognized. It is severed and will remain severed, probably forever, from its parent world. Its men hold no communication with us, and it is long since we have heard how they fared. A conspiracy of silence has closed down on its unfortunate existence, and one of our earliest – though involuntary – settlements is unknown to most Earthmen even by name. Its story is unique.

I

MISADVENTURE

A violent shock threw the navigator of the *Argenta* forward in his chair so that he sprawled across his control desk. His two companions in the navigating dome staggered and slid across the deck plates. The clangour of a dozen or more alarm bells jangled throughout the ship. Angus McDowell, the chief engineer, made his way back to the desk, ruefully rubbing that part of his head which had met the wall.

'What the hell – ?' he began in a mildly surprised tone. The third man, Joe Seely, scrambling from the floor, cut him short.

'Holed, sure as we're living,' he exclaimed. 'These ruddy asteroids! – where's the damage, David ?'

The navigator turned to look up at the rows of indicators mounted to the left of his desk. In the middle of the top row a red light was winking briskly.

'Guard room,' he reported.

'Hell!' Joe, who was officer of the watch, tore out of the navigating dome and they could hear his voice bellowing orders down the corridor as he ran. Angus strolled closer to the desk. His was a lanky, angular figure possessed of long arms and big joints. He showed no smoothly rounded muscular development, but those who had once tried conclusions with his tough, sinewy frame seldom wished for more. A long faced Scotchman, this, who had never known Scotland. The product of ancestors bred in the shipyards of the Clyde; inheriting their engineering tradition with their blood. His manner towards the navigator was slightly paternal.

'Serious, Sonny ?' he asked.

David shrugged his shoulders. A few years in the service had already given him a degree of that fatalism characteristic of so many space sailors.

'Final for those who happened to be in the guard room. That indicator means that they hadn't a chance to plug the leak. All their air was gone in two seconds. For the ship as a whole, not very serious'.

Angus nodded relievedly. 'Surprising it wasn't my engines.

We do have a bit of luck – sometimes.' He paused before he added: 'Think I'll cut along and have a look at the mess.'

Angus clattered across the room, bending his head as he passed through the low exit. David returned to his calculations and corrections. No one was to blame for the accident. Approaching the asteroid belt, above the plane of the ecliptic, one could do no more than plot a course avoiding the larger, known fragments of rock, and trust to luck for the rest. Luck, on this occasion, had been less unkind than she frequently was.

Angus, making his way forward, toward the guard room, found a knot of men crowded around the entrance. Above the door, now automatically sealed by air pressure, a red danger light glowed steadily. Joe Seely was, with some difficulty, climbing into a space-suit and attempting to bawl his orders above the continued clamour of the alarms. As the bells abruptly ceased Angus heard him say:

'Six men to bring the portable airlock. Snap to it.'

The six raced off down the passageway while he still struggled with the intractable garment. When, at last, the stiff folds had been tugged up and the fasteners securely fixed, he picked up the air tanks and examined the dials. He dropped them disgustedly.

'Half pressure – criminal carelessness. Somebody's in for it over this. You!' he roared, startling a near member of the crew, 'new oxygen pack. Jump to it!'

He lifted the space helmet and, turning it over between his hands, examined it with caution.

'Hm. Appears to be satisfactory,' he admitted grudgingly.

Angus with a grin placed his big hand on the other's shoulder.

'Now, don't you get rattled, laddie,' he advised. 'Gettin' rattled never did a man any good. He forgets details if he gets all het up – and you only forget details once when you're in space.'

For a moment Joe seemed inclined to resent the warning. Then he smiled back and nodded. Angus was an oldtimer and privileged. Besides, he had spoken the truth: Joe had been getting windy.

The party returned bearing the portable airlock. It was in the form of a hollow box built of steelium sheets, but it lacked one of the longer sides. Around the six feet by four of this missing part, it was heavily faced with rubber. In the side opposite the space was set a door. The men fitted the contrivance over the guard room door so that side flanges slid over bolts provided for the purpose. While they worked hard with spanners to secure it, another of the crew attached the pipe which would later exhaust the air. Joe watched fidgeting impatiently until the spanners were laid aside.

'Finished?'

'All correct, sir,' the leader assured him.

'Good. Give me a hand with this helmet.'

Half a minute later he was inside the lock. He made sure that all was in order and the door safely bolted behind him and gave the starting signal of three taps on the metal wall. The pointer before him began to back swiftly as the pump did its work. In a short time the pressure became low enough for him to open the guard room door and, with a rush, the remaining air dissipated into the vacuum.

Joe moved clumsily over the threshold and surveyed the room. It was not a pleasant sight. It was, in fact, far worse than he had expected. For one thing there had evidently been far more men in the room than was usual at any one time. Their lifeless bodies seemed everywhere. Sagging in their chairs, fallen forward across the tables or sprawled on the floor wherever the sudden going of the air had left them. Their faces were grey-blue and their mouths lolled open to show grey tongues.

Their fingers were tight clenched as though in a last, despairing clutch at receding life, and their eyes, fantastically protruding, seemed still to stare at death. The eyes of some had left their sockets. From the noses and ears of many, little streams of blood had spurted to be frozen by the cold of space. Joe felt sick. It was not the first time he had seen men dead from exposure to the vacuum, but it was the first time he had seen them in such numbers.

He counted more than thirty – almost the entire corps of guards snuffed out in a single moment. For what purpose they had all been assembled at once, he could not guess. He pulled himself together and brought his mind back to the practical aspect of the situation.

'It'll be tough work looking after the prisoners now,' he muttered.

He looked along the room and saw on the port side the three-foot hole which had caused the tragedy. Beyond, he could look out into space – a velvet blackness, pricked by distant stars. He turned to starboard in search of the corresponding hole and saw with a shock that there was none. He had never heard of a meteorite failing to pass clean through any ship it had struck. It became plain that here was a chance in several million. The object must have been moving at a speed but little different from their own. Its force at the angle of impact had only, therefore, been sufficient to carry it through one side of the *Argenta*. A short search for the cause of the mischief revealed it lying beside one of the corpses at the foot of a stanchion. The stanchion, massive member though it was, had been badly bent by the encounter. Joe whistled softly in surprise as he looked down. Instead of the irregular lump of cosmic rubbish he expected, he found himself gazing at a dented, steelium cylinder.

'A message rocket,' he muttered. 'Now what the – ?'

Bending down, he rolled it over and felt for the catch which would slide the message compartment cover aside. He found it and gave the necessary combined pressure and twist. The lid snapped back to reveal only a single sheet of paper which he snatched up hurriedly and stuffed into a pocket of his space-suit.

After a few more minutes of cursory examination of the room, he crossed to the wall and lifted down one of the emergency plates which must be carried in all rooms and cabins. Leaving this handy, he returned to the doorway and gave the signal taps for the admission of air. Then he hurried back to the plate and held it over the hole waiting for the air pressure to lock it into position with a weight of fifteen pounds to the square inch. It could not keep out the cold of space for the vacuum in that section of the double hull had been destroyed, but it would keep in the air and artificial warmth could be supplied for the time taken in repairs.

Some little time passed without result. Evidently there had been a hitch somewhere and again Joe began to grumble over the inefficiency of the *Argenta's* crew as he waited for the valve to open. At last, however, the needle of the wall dial flickered and began slowly to turn. Soon it became unnecessary for him to hold the emergency plate. He turned off his air supply and removed his helmet as the pointer neared the fifteen mark. Then he strode over to the door of the lock. He began to speak angrily as he opened it, but the words died as he stared at a pistol ominously facing him.

'Both hands up, please,' said a voice quietly.

His helmet fell with a crash as his hands rose.

II

REVOLT

Joe emerged from the lock and looked wonderingly around the semi-circle of facing men. They were short, large-chested men with brown faces and hands. The meaning of the situation struck him with an unpleasant jolt.

'The Martians – the prisoners,' he exclaimed.

Thus did the widespread Martian revolt of 2077 affect even the *Argenta*, far out in space.

The man who held the pistol answered Joe.

'The Martians, yes, but it is you Earthmen who are the prisoners now.' His speech was both good and fluent though, like that of most of his race, he retained the characteristic lilt.

Joe could see Angus at the rear of the group, towering over his lessor captors. The Scotchman was manifesting no little irritation:

'– lot of lousy sons of misbegotten desert rats. You'll see what you'll get for this, you – ugh.' The speech ended in a grunt as a pistol jabbed uncomfortably in his ribs. Joe turned back to his captor.

'This is piracy. You know the penalty?'

The Martian smiled. 'This is more than mere piracy – it is revolution. Everywhere the Martians are turning upon their oppressors. You thought that we were crushed. You thought that you had stamped out the last spark of our spirit when at length you caught Sen-Su and condemned him and us to exile. That was a foolish thing to do. Our plans were already made. By the arrest of Sen-Su you gained us more support and lit the fuse of the revolution. Every loyal Martian knew the date and the time.'

As he finished, another group approached down the corridor. Joe could see that it comprised most of the ship's officers including David Robbins, the navigator. One, however, he missed.

16

'Where is Captain Briscoe?'

'Unfortunately, he is dead.' admitted the Martian.

'If you killed him, you swine –' began Angus.

The other shook his head.

'We did not. He succeeded in killing two of us, but when he saw that we had really got the situation in hand, he shot himself. It was a great pity. There would have been no dishonour for him to surrender.'

Joe believed him. He knew the old captain for a man of dogged pride; incapable of surrender while the means of death remained.

'And what's to be done with us?' he asked, hoping his uneasiness was not audible in his voice.

'For the present you will be confined in the officer's mess. Your crew is now occupying our cells.'

By this time the two groups had joined and were moving on together. At the door of the mess room they halted. Each of the seven officers was first searched for concealed weapons and then passed in. Finally the door was closed and bolted upon a very dejected group of men. Only Angus retained the spirit to express his opinion of the situation: it appeared to amount to a withering blast of non-repetitive profanity.

'All right, all right,' counselled Joe after a while. At another time he might have admired Angus' linguistic attainments, but at present they seemed unhelpful. 'Just forget the Martians' ancestors for a bit – they're dead, anyway. The trouble is, what're we going to do? We can't sit down under this.'

'Do? What the hell can we do? I don't mind telling you it's the last time I ship on a ruddy convict carrier. What sort of filthy mess are they making of my engines, I wonder? A lot of stinking, bladder-chested –'

'Oh, cut it out. Have we got any weapons?'

David jerked open a drawer which he remembered to have contained a pair of pistols. It was empty. A search of the room soon revealed that the Martians had been over it in anticipation of their hopes.

'Hm, they're no fools.' Joe noticed the door at the other end of the room. 'Try that door, David.'

David walked across and rattled the handle vainly. He shook his head.

'They seem to have caught us properly,' he admitted.

'What puzzles me is how they worked it. They can't have known that we were going to be holed.'

'No. That must have been just luck,' Joe agreed. 'Judging from what the man with the gun said, it was all pre-arranged. The guards being wiped out meant that they caught us sitting instead of having to fight. But I'd like to know just how they got out.'

As he spoke, he had been unfastening the space-suit which still encumbered him. He struggled awkwardly out of it and threw it into a corner. Torrence, the first officer, had made no comment since the calamity. Now he began to speak. Since the death of the captain, he became senior officer and, therefore, in command; none of those present had seemed to appreciate this, and his tone showed his resentment. He was unfortunate in that a peremptory knocking at the door cut him short halfway through the first sentence. All the men turned surprisedly. This seemed an unusual courtesy to prisoners.

'Unbolt this door at once,' demanded a Martian voice while its owner rattled the handle.

David was about to call out that it was already unbolted, but, at a sign from Angus, he stopped. The Scotchman rose swiftly from his chair and lifted it above his head. He crossed the room and posted himself behind the door.

'It's not bolted,' he called.

He braced himself, ready to crash the chair upon the head of the first comer. The rest prepared to spring for the fallen man's weapon and charge the door.

Disconcertingly, a voice addressed them from behind.

'Ah,' it said, 'a little reception committee. I thought there might be, so I took the precaution of entering by the other door.'

They all whipped round to face a Martian who was accompanied by armed guards. Angus shamefacedly lowered his chair. The newcomer was short, even for his race, but his proportions were excellent, and in his carriage was a dignity utterly different from the frequent pomposity of small men. A slight smile crossed his clean-cut face at the sight of their surprise.

'A little ruse of mine,' he explained.

'Who are you, and what do you want?' Torrence demanded curtly.

'My name, probably familiar to you, is Sen-Su. Till lately I was one of your prisoners.'

18

'The Martian nationalist?'

'Yes, and no doubt you have all heard many unpleasant things about me – probably are wondering what particular form of torment I have in store for you. They have made quite a bogy of me on Earth; I assure you they exaggerate. It has been a Governmental policy to malign me – Governments have to create thorough-going villains. In private life we should call them liars, but in public life they are propagandists.'

'Well?' Torrence attempted to make it clear from his tone that he was prepared to waste very little breath and time with a man of an inferior race.

'I have come primarily to express my regret at the death of Captain Briscoe. I assure you I regard it as a serious stain on an otherwise successful coup.'

There was no immediate reply from the Earthmen. They had not been taught to believe that Martians held to such a standard of behaviour. In fact, it was frequently stated that no Martian knew the meaning of the word "honour." David studied the little brown man and saw sincerity in his eyes. There was no mistaking the real thing. Moreover, many times in the past he had doubted that the Martians were such scum as Earth, in general, credited them with being. He looked around at his silent comrades and took it upon himself to reply.

'We thank you for that,' he said.

Angus, after a puzzled stare leaned over towards him.

'I believe you're right, Sonny,' he confided in a hoarse whisper. 'He means it.'

Torrence cut in with a sharp demand to know Sen-Su's intentions. The other raised his eyebrows at the tone, but his voice remained even as he answered:

'That is simple. Our parts are reversed. For you, the fate which was to be ours: for us, the occupations which were yours.'

'You intend to maroon us on the planetoid, Asperus?'

As Sen-Su nodded Torrence broke out wrathfully:

'You won't get away with that. All the ships in the Solar system will be at your heels. Far better surrender quietly now.'

Sen-Su smiled again, tolerantly.

'I see you do not yet understand. This is no isolated reversal for Earth. It is a fight for liberty. Everywhere, save on Earth itself, Martians have by this time risen in thousands, determined as only a persecuted people can be, to end Earth's oppression. You came to Mars and found an old race – old, before yours began. We were prepared to be friendly, but you let loose your adolescent cruelty upon us. You could not understand that a people may outgrow the futilities of war and strife. You called us decadent and weak.

'This impression, coloured with fictitious stories of our vices, was suggested again and again to all Earthmen, and, such is the immense power of suggestion scientifically sustained we became to your minds, monsters of depravity. The truth – that we were an old race, resting as a man rests when his work is done – was not allowed to percolate into your thoughts. You have disturbed our content; stirred us from our peace, and your oppression has meant our rejuvenation. Old Mars has had to arise in all her ancient might against alien barbarians.'

The first officer stepped forward with fists clenched.

'Barbarians ? *You* call *us* barbarians ?'

Pistols waved him back. Sen-Su shrugged his shoulders.

'If a demonstration of barbarity were needed, you have given it. You react like an animal.'

'But you cannot hope to subdue Earth and all her millions,' Joe objected. 'For one thing, there are not enough of you.'

'True. And that is not our intention. For one thing, it would be as barbarous as your treatment of us. We merely refuse to let ourselves and our planet be further exploited for one-sided gain. Now, I will leave you – I have important matters to attend to. I trust that I have made the situation clearer.'

The Martian party retired leaving an astounded group of prisoners behind them. The situation had indeed been made unpleasantly clear. Sen-Su's manner and restraint in itself had been a shock to men who had been taught to consider all Martians as mere semi-civilized degenerates who should be thankful to Earthmen for introducing the strong hand of control. His moderation was a contradiction of all their schooling. Torrence expressed his ill-controlled anger in threats. Angus, for once, was silent. He looked thoughtful.

'You know, Sonny,' he remarked after a while to David, 'I've got a feeling that there's a deal in what the man said.'

David nodded his agreement.

'I know. I've got that feeling, too. Of course, we always have been told what swine the Martians are, but how much of that is just politics? Has any of us here ever really known the Martians?'

Torrence looked across and became conscious again of his position as first officer. His anger, moreover, had not abated.

'So that's the way of the wind? Not only is our ship seized by pirates and our captain killed, but we have traitors among our own officers.' His voice was truculent. 'Well, we know how to deal with traitors, don't we, boys?'

He looked around as he finished the question, but the response was curiously half-hearted. Most of the men turned their gaze aside rather than meet his. Angus stared at him with a pair of cold, hard eyes.

'You're a fool – but for that, I'd knock your rotten teeth and your insults down your throat together. I'm every bit as much against the Martians as you are, but that's no reason for fooling myself with a deck of lies.'

'You're calling me a liar?' Torrence rose.

'It seems to me we've all been hearing or telling lies about Mars, but that doesn't say I'm backing the Martians. If somebody in the Solar System has to get a bad deal, I'm still going to do my best to see it's not Earth.'

'You were talking sedition,' Torrence retorted doggedly. 'You and Robbins, there. As senior officer it is my duty –'

Angus had crossed and stood over the other, his long arms swinging ready.

'Your duty is what? You miserable little half-baked, wooden-headed –'

Joe Seely hurried to intervene. He swiftly retrieved the paper he had stowed in the space-suit pocket and waved it at the rest.

'Say, here's a bit of news for you,' he called loudly. 'That thing that broke into the guard room wasn't a meteorite – it was a message rocket.'

They all turned incredulously. Message rockets, as they all very well knew, had been banned by government decree for over twenty years.

'You mean to say the thing lodged aboard us?' David asked.

'I do, and here's the message.'

Joe unfolded the paper carefully and laid it on the mess table. The others, forgetful of the brewing fight, came clustering round him.

'The fellow who invented those things ought to have been

sent off in one himself,' said Angus. 'It's a safe bet they've wrecked more ships than they've ever saved.' He leaned over Joe's shoulder and peered down at the sheet.

The date at the head was the fourteenth of August in the year 2052 A. D. – twenty-five years ago. For that quarter of a century the message rocket, having missed its objective, had been floating aimlessly in space, to end by causing the death of thirty and more good men. It was no wonder the devices had been banned. The message was brief, but plain:

"Rocket ship, RED GLORY *(C.O.* 1009), *passenger liner bound from Earth to the Moons of Jupiter. Disabled in the asteroid belt, and wrecked by forced landing upon planetoid believed to be Asperus. 300 survivors. Radio out of commission. Send help."*

The signature at the foot read: '*James Stuart (Captain)*'.

Angus bent down to look more closely and assure himself that there was no mistake.

'Old Jamie, by the Lord. It's a small system. Does anyone remember a rescue from Asperus ?'

No one did.

'Then it's odds on he's there still – if he's alive.'

'If they navigate properly, we should make Asperus in a couple of days,' remarked David. 'And, by the look of things at present, we'll have plenty of time to make a search.'

III

ON ASPERUS

The imprisoned officers crowded to the windows as the *Argenta* slowed for landing by circling about Asperus. The planetoid, although larger than Eros, had been discovered later, possibly because its orbit is almost circular while Eros, travelling his very oval path comes close to the Earth at times. Another difference between them is that Asperus is a spherical body while Eros, strangely enough, is not.

The name, 'Asperus', denotes, as it should, a world craggy and broken to the last degree of roughness, but it carries also a suggestion of barren severity which is entirely misplaced. On the contrary, vegetation is profuse.

As they watched the tumbled landscape far beneath, David gave such scraps of information as he could dig out of his memory. The diameter, he told them, was just under five hundred miles, though the density of the core was many times greater than that of Earth. The period of rotation was almost exactly twelve hours, and its year, 1,600 earth-days in length. Geographically he could tell only that it possessed two large seas, much broken with islands. But the men paid him little attention, they were far too interested in examining for themselves the world which must support them for an indefinite length of time.

Profuse is an inadequate word to describe the vegetation which clothes this pocket planet. They could see all the land wrapped in a green blanket from which, here and there, only the craggiest of spires pierced upwards in their rocky nakedness. Foliage sprang from every pocket of soil, bushes waved atop the most unlikely peaks and festoons of swaying creepers hung down from the ledges like green waterfalls pouring into the still denser growths below. Occasional gleams of water showed where steep-sided clefts had succeeded in trapping miniature lakes, and, infrequently, there occurred larger, shadowed valleys which could show level ground dotted with not inconsiderable trees. As the *Argenta* swept nearer still, a half-checked exclamation burst from Angus. He pressed closer to the window.

'What is it?' asked Joe, beside him.

But Angus made no reply. For the present he was keeping to himself the knowledge of a bright, metallic glint which had flashed from one valley. He marked the spot mentally by the queerly twisted crag which dominated it.

The ship, now travelling slowly, searched for a landing. A few moments later she was sinking gently to a green spread berth. Joe voiced the general sentiment as they touched.

'Well, we might be in a worse hole. There's certainly no desert here like there is on most of Eros. Even the mountains don't seem so high when you get the right proportions – nothing like Earth's mountains although they're so broken.'

Doctor Cleary, the medical officer, surveyed the scene less kindly. It would probably, he thought, mean a lot of work for him; this transferring of species to an alien world was not always the simple matter it appeared. But he made no comment; optimistic men are healthier than pessimists.

An audible bustling began to take place about the ship. There came a clang as the exit ramp was lowered. They watched the twenty-eight members of the crew march out under an escort of armed Martians, and turned sharply as the door of the mess room was flung open.

'This way!' ordered a sing-song voice.

They were conducted first to their cabins where it was permitted, under supervision, to collect such personal belongings as they might wish to take, and thence to the open. Sen-Su, personally supervising the explusion, regarded them negligently as they passed him, but as they stepped off the ramp, he gazed more intently and a line appeared between his brows.

'Fu-Tan,' he called, 'how many officers are present?'

'Six, sir.'

'There should be seven.'

The man addressed as Fu-Tan looked puzzled for a moment, then:

'The tall man, the engineer, is missing,' he said.

'Find him at once.'

It was a mystery how Angus had managed to slip away. Neither the Martians nor his companions had noticed his going. Fu-Tan raised his lilting voice in orders. The business of unloading supplies for the exiles was suspended while all but a handful of guards joined in the hunt. It proved brief, for the *Argenta* was deficient in good hiding places. An approaching hubbub in the corridors soon suggested that the escaper had been caught; muffled broadsides of blistering blasphemy tended to confirm the suggestion. Angus, still muttering and cursing, appeared at the head of the ramp and was hustled down. Sen-Su smiled at his angry face.

'No stowaways on my ship,' he said.

Angus' reply was unprintable, but had the other looked a little more closely he might have discerned an unaccountable gleam in the engineer's eyes.

The unloading of food and medical supplies was resumed. Reports on Asperus stated that edible fruits grew abundantly so that the preserved food was more of a luxury than a necessity. When all the cases had been stacked, each man was given a broad-bladed, razor-edged knife some eighteen inches long.

The guards filed back into the ship. The ramp was withdrawn and its covering port made firm. A preliminary roar came from the rocket tubes. The *Argenta* lifted a trifle by the bows, then, with a blast of power, she was gone, climbing on a steep slant into the heavens. Gloomily the stranded Earthmen watched her shrink.

'Well, it can't be for long,' said David, at length. 'Once they find that Sen-Su's in circulation again, they'll realize what's happened and send for us.'

'And a pretty pack of fools we'll look,' returned Joe. 'The marooners marooned . . . What the devil's the matter with you ?'

Angus, to whom the last part of the remark was addressed, was emitting a series of explosive grunts, suspiciously like laughter.

'Well, for a queer sense of humour, commend me to a Scot. What's so damned funny about this, I'd like to know ?'

Angus got a hold on himself. 'Sen-Su thinks he's marooned us.'

'Not a bad think, either.'

'Yes, but he can't get away. I wasn't trying to stow away. I got along and opened the draining valves. He's not got enough fuel left to get clear. Our job was to dump him and his bunch, and we've done it in spite of them.'

'I'll be . . . So that was your little game. Angus, you're a genius.' Joe slapped him on the back.

The spirits of the whole company rose. Even though they had lost their ship and had been stranded, Angus had saved them from falling down on the main job. After a hurried discussion, it was decided to put some distance between themselves and the valley. When the Martians should notice their supply dials, it was considered likely that they would head back there, and no one was anxious to try conclusions with a shipload of angry Martians. The next question arose over the direction to be taken.

'I suppose one way's as good as another ?' asked Joe.

'No,' Angus advised. 'Down to the south of this I saw something as we came over, and I'm willing to bet it was the wreck of the *Red Glory* or some other ship.'

'Taking a lot on yourselves, aren't you ?' suggested Torrence. 'I'd just like to remind you again that I am in command here.' He looked round to see how this information was received. The men's expressions told him little. No one wished to mutiny, but if it came to a choice of leadership between a man promoted through influence, and one who had roughed the ether for many a year, they knew which to prefer. Joe Seely set himself to manage a tactful interposition with the result that the party moved to the south under the nominal leadership of the first officer, and the practical guidance of Angus.

Travel across Asperus was a curious sensation for Earth-bred men. Those with experience of planetary exploration managed to adapt themselves in short time to the low gravitation, but the novices continued to overshoot their aims again and again before they learned to gauge truly the amount of effort required. It was exasperating for these tyros to be carried sailing past their objectives by ill-judged bounds, but there was little danger of harm since descent seemed a matter of floating down rather than of falling. For half an hour Angus set a stiff pace, launching in a series of powerful leaps over such country as would have baffled all but the most skilful climbers had they had to contend with earthly gravitation. He noticed that the mountains were pitted with frequent caves, some obscured by screens of bushes and creepers, but others showing as stark, black holes in naked rock faces. The thought struck him that they might prove useful hiding places in case of pursuit. There was some grumbling from the rear about the unnecessary speed, but Angus knew what he was about. He was convinced that the *Argenta* would make for the valley where she had set them down, and his ears were wide open.

At the first mutter of distant rockets he gave the order to take cover and they crouched in the bushes, watching the ship as she swung like a silver shuttle above them. She sank slowly down behind crags they had already crossed. Angus gave the 'all-clear,' and moved on in fantastic, flying leaps towards the south.

Night fell with surprising suddenness. Angus had hoped to reach the wreck while daylight lasted, but Asperus' swift revolution whisked the shrunken, distant sun out of sight while the rugged landmark was still several miles ahead. They were left without light save for the sheen of accompanying asteroids and the glimmer of far-off constellations, almost unaltered. Travel over such country became well-nigh impossible.

Torrence suggested that the short night should be spent in one of the many caves, and Angus offered no objection. They had secured a good lead over the Martians and, even were their trail to be discovered, little or nothing could be done until dawn. One of the men reported a large cavern a few yards back. Torrence found it and led them into the gloom; his sword-like knife ready to his hand.

Angus struck a match, carefully shielding its rays from the entrance. By the flicker they could see a floor some twelve feet across and so dry as to be dusty, stretching back into the body of the mountain until it became lost in the blackness. The sides curved up into an arched roof five feet above their heads.

'Excellent!' pronounced Torrence briskly. 'It is dry, the entrance is not likely to be discovered and it is easily defensible.'

Angus started to speak and then restrained himself. The first officer was touchy and would certainly take any objection as a new attempt to belittle his dignity. Nevertheless, the engineer was uneasy though he would have been hard put to adduce any reason for his misgiving. Perhaps he had inherited a lingering fear of those hobgoblins and gnomes who had, according to legend, so sorely harassed his Celtic ancestors. Whatever the reason, it caused him to lie close to the entrance. Soon the sense of disquiet passed and he, like the rest, save for the sentry at the cave mouth, was asleep.

He awoke with a start. His hand already gripping the knife by his side. From somewhere came the whispering swish of a faint, ghostly movement. He looked towards the entrance and half started up. The sentry was no longer standing silhouetted on the ledge. A faint shuffling on the other side brought him round, trying vainly to pierce the wall of darkness. Stealthily he drew his feet up and settled the long knife more firmly in his hand. A scrape and the clatter of a loose stone jerked his head back to the entrance, and he drew a sudden breath. Black figures were stirring; indistinct outlines against the dark sky. Moving shadows: not the short Martians he had half expected, but grotesque, shrouded figures, six feet and more in height.

A SUDDEN DISCOVERY

It was no time for inquiry; the vanished sentry told enough. Already a pair of the creatures were within the entrance. He could see them bending ominously above his sleeping friends. With whirling knife he leapt silently upon them. He felt the keen edge bite home and, simultaneously, there came a cry. A scream, but a scream no human throat could give; a mournful ululation with a harsh stridency which shredded the silence.

Confusion broke loose. The men sprang up, startled, yet bemused with sleep, and groping for their knives. The black prowlers retreated before Angus' circling blade, making headlong for the open. Twice more he felt the steel cleave deep before he gained the cave-mouth. The air sang in his ears with the shrill screams of alarmed and injured creatures.

He saw a half-dozen launch themselves into space as he came out upon the rocky ledge. Black forms which fell for a moment and then spread monstrous wings to check the fall. He watched them move in slow, powerful beats as the creatures rose and banked. Not for an instant did they check their desolate cries. Harshly the sound echoed in the shadow-hidden valley beneath and from further and yet further crags sprang answering cries like the wailing of funereal despair. A crescendo of screeching lament tortured the still night to pandemonium.

Mixed with the shrilling came the hoarser cries of striving men. Behind Angus a crowd of milling figures struggled and slashed in the dark, combating invisible opponents. With a stentorian command he dispersed the panic of their rough awakening and shook them into reality. They lowered their weapons and stood alert, breathing hard. From the dark, mysterious tunnel behind came the sounds of hurried feet mingled with those of occasional cries eerily echoing against the walls; sounds which grew fainter as their makers fled into the rocky heart of the mountain.

'What – what were they?' Torrence's dignity had fallen away and his voice was shaky.

Angus made no reply. Instead, he struck a light and counted the white, startled faces about him.

'Twenty-seven.'

Nobody commented, but a number of heads turned to let their owners gaze fearfully into the blackness whither two officers and six men had passed to an unknown fate.

'And Davie, and the rest are at the mercy of these blasted things – whatever they are,' growled Angus.

With the dawn they were able to examine the bodies of two of the assailants Angus had felled. They were bipeds, and that together with the disposition of organs common to most mammals, gave the impression that they were at least semi-human. Other characteristics did their best to counteract the impression. The creatures were a dull, metallic grey in colour, tall, thin and fragilely made. Attenuated arms, so long as to reach almost to the feet, were linked to the legs by enormous spans of membranous wings. Their only weapons appeared as cruelly curved claws at both the fore and hind tips of the wings. The size and shape of their half-human heads seemed to suggest an intelligence of some order. High enough, at least, to embarrass seriously a small party armed only with knives.

Nevertheless, Angus wished to lead a rescue party. He was dissuaded only with difficulty. The others managed, at last, to convice him that it would be more than foolhardy under the circumstances to attempt the exploration of the unlit caverns containing unknown numbers of the winged creatures. David Robbins, Doctor Cleary and the six men with them must be abandoned for the present, at least. When – and if – they should discover the *Red Glory*, they would have a stronghold, and – they hoped – weapons.

'The best thing we can do now,' said Joe, in conclusion, 'is to get right along, before those Martians get busy. They're sure to be on our tracks after that hullaballoo last night. We've got to settle with them before we can get a line on these flying screechers – the betting is that our men are safe for a while, if they're not dead already.'

For an hour Angus led on, leaping prodigiously, climbing and scrambling through valleys choked with foliage and up precipices whose faces were hidden behind thick tresses of creeper. If he had any doubt of the direction, any uncertainty, no suspicion of it was allowed to appear. They paused only once. Beside a stream in one of the lesser valleys, a man caught his foot in something which rattled drily. He jumped back with a cry which caused the rest to stop short.

'What is it?' Joe called.

'A skeleton, sir,' the man reported.

Joe came back. He saw at a glance that the bleached bones were human. Tangled among the ribs, he caught a glint of metal and drew out a slender chain on which swung an identity disc.

'Will Fording, Chicago, Radio Operator, *Red Glory*, (C.O. 1009),' he read.

He picked up the rifle which lay beside the remains. It was utterly useless and caked in the rust of many years' accumulation.

'Poor devil – wonder what got him?' he murmured.

He dropped the gun and slipped the identity disc in his pocket. The party went on its way slightly chastened. So far they had encountered no sign of native animal life beyond the grey creatures and a few insects. The radio operator might have died of sickness or accident – it was impossible to guess with the little they knew of this queer planetoid.

An hour later, they breasted the final rocky ridge to gaze down on a sight which brought excited exclamations from them all. Close to the far side of a valley somewhat larger than any they had yet encountered lay a space ship of antiquated design. Her untarnishable plates still glittered in the sunlight, but half surrounding her were deep growths of a sturdiness which told that it was many years since she had sunk to this, her final, berth.

Angus' sharp eyes picked out the name *Red Glory* inscribed in faded letters upon her prow; beneath, half obscured by branches, he could make out a part of her Chicago registration number. But it was not the sight of the ship which had caused the party's surprise. They had expected no less. Their exclamations were due to the fact that the undergrowth before the entrance port had been cleared away. A broad path led from the ship to several acres of cultivated plots beside the stream which wandered down the centre of the valley.

Joe, for one, felt a rush of relief. Since the previous night's encounter he had been aware of growing doubts that any of the *Red Glory's* complement could have survived.

'*Red Glory*, ahoy,' yelled Angus.

No voice replied though he fancied he saw a flicker of movement at one of the cabin windows. There was no wave of a welcoming arm such as he had expected. They hastened down the steep wall and across the valley floor. Midway up the cleared track to the open port, a voice called them to halt. Before and behind them figures oddly clad in rough materials stepped from the concealing bushes. All were men, and all held rifles trained upon them. A young man – Angus estimated his age at twenty-three or four – stepped forward and approached with wary suspicion.

'Who are you, and where do you come from?' he asked.

Torrence replied, and the young man watched him intently as he spoke. He seemed slightly at a loss. As he began to reply a figure made its appearance in the entrance of the *Red Glory*. An old man who stooped, and whose white hair hung down upon the shoulders of his coarse woven coat, but who still gazed with keen eyes from a weather beaten face.

'Jamie!' cried Angus. 'Jamie, don't you know me?'

The old man's face cracked into a smile.

'Aye, Angus, lad, it's you all right. Come along in and bring your friends with you.'

With one hand he waved away the riflemen who appeared bewildered, but retreated obediently.

'Well I'll be damned,' muttered Joe, 'does he think we've just dropped in to supper?'

Angus grinned.

'You could never surprise old Jamie – no one ever has.'

Accompanied by the riflemen who had not entirely lost their suspicion, the party filed aboard the ship.

They entered the main living room to see a group of girls arranging baskets of strange Asperian fruits on the tables.

'Ye'll be wantin' some food, I doubt,' said Jamie. 'And ye can talk while ye eat. We heard your rockets yesterday,' he continued. 'The first rockets I've heard in twenty-five years – man, it was grand; like music.'

As the tale of the *Argenta* was told, more and more men and women and a number of children came crowding into the room. With some surprise Joe noticed the predominance of youth. There might have been perhaps thirty persons of middle age, and a few besides Jamie of advanced years, but the rest fell, almost without exception, below the twenty-four level. A number of them were introduced including the suspicious young man who had waylaid them. He, it transpired, was Andrew Stuart, son of old Jamie. Greta, one of the most attractive of the girls, was his wife.

Jamie heard their story through with little comment, but at the end he called Andrew to him and directed that a scouting party should be sent out. He looked a little worried as he turned back.

'We've got to keep these Martians away,' he said. ''Tis a pretty situation – they've got a good ship and no fuel, while we've got a useless ship, but there's plenty of fuel in her tanks yet.'

'Have you got rifles for us?' asked Angus.

'Aye, and pistols – more than we can use.'

Angus looked surprised, but a look in the old man's eye checked his question. He decided that Jamie had been doing a little gun-running as a sideline, and would not relish inquiries. Instead, he asked:

'What about your story? And what about these flying things? We're all sort of mazed.'

Jamie began his history from the disablement of the *Red Glory*. They had run into a meteor shower and had been lucky in not being carved to bits. Happily most of their score of leaks had been small, but the radio had been demolished and the relief operator who was in the room at the time, killed. One mixing chamber for gases had been wrecked, putting a number of tubes out of action.

They had set about limping for the nearest approaching body which they had believed to be Asperus. And, thanks to the low pull of the planetoid, managed a successful, if ungraceful landing. Thereafter a number of message rockets had been dispatched without result. The exact number of survivors, including passengers and crew, had been three hundred and seven.

In those first days Asperus had seemed a not unkindly place. It produced the necessities of life in abundance, and there was a feeling that fate might have been far more severe. Then, a week after the landing, fifty of their number, many of them women, disappeared. A search party was sent out and never seen again. Up to this time they had seen nothing of the grey, winged creatures which they later came to call by the name of 'Batrachs.' A second search party met a similar fate and still more of the survivors disappeared until, at last, Jamie had taken a firm stand.

Every sunset the door of the *Red Glory* was closed and locked and remained thus until dawn; nobody, under any circumstances, being permitted to go out by night. The numbers had now been reduced to sixty-five, omitting children. The Batrachs made bolder by their captures had besieged the ship for several nights, but, finding it impregnable, at last abandoned the practice. For several years now no member of the *Red Glory* colony had set eyes on a Batrach.

The creatures were strictly nocturnal in their surface operations, and the men became no less strictly diurnal. From that time the little colony had begun to prosper. Jamie from his position as captain had slid to the status of patriarchal ruler.

'But these Batrachs?' inquired Angus. 'You had guns to fight them with?'

'Yes, we had guns,' Jamie nodded, 'but so had the expeditions and they never came back. After all, laddie, a gun, even if it fires rocket shells, is at a disadvantage in the dark, and the Batrachs don't come in ones or twos, but in thousands. You were lucky last night; the only reason you are here now is that they didn't expect you. If they had been prepared –' He spread expressive hands and shook his head.

V

TO THE RESCUE

Sometimes, Jamie admitted, he had thought of leading out yet another search party, but it was his duty to stay with his ship and protect the survivors to the best of his ability. There had been marriages. Jamie, as captain, had performed them, even his own. He had now become, he said proudly, not only the father of two boys and two girls, but a grandfather as well. The Batrachs, in his opinion were the only unhealthy things about Asperus; all the children of the colony had flourished though he considered them slightly underdeveloped muscularly by reason of the lesser gravitation.

Angus, seeing that the story was tending to become a family history, pulled him back to the subject of Batrachs. Couldn't Jamie give more details about them? What did they do with their prisoners ? What was their level of intelligence ? Did they ever use weapons ? He extracted little. Jamie considered them almost equal to men in intelligence – save that they never used weapons; of their treatment of prisoners he could say nothing, for no one had ever returned to tell. His tone showed plainly that he thought no one would, but Angus had different ideas on that subject.

Talk was cut short by the return of a scout who reported that the Martians were encamping in the next valley. Thoughts of rescue were temporarily put aside. Sen-Su and his little lot must be settled first.

First officer Torrence again emerged from that oblivion to which events seemed to condemn him. He proposed a sniping party. The suggestion met with a cold reception which genuinely astonished him. Angus was particularly incensed.

'This is not a murder gang. Our orders did not extend beyond marooning a bunch of political prisoners. They didn't ill treat us when we were at their mercy –'

'They're nothing more than a lot of damned pirates, and the penalty for piracy is death.'

Angus kept his temper with difficulty.

'That's as may be. If they had been real pirates, we'd now be so many corpses floating out there in space. I, for one, refuse to shoot them down in cold blood. They treated us well.'

'They murdered Captain Briscoe.'

'That's a lie!'

'This is mutiny.' Torrence's eyes were gleaming. He turned as though to appeal to old Jamie, but Angus cut him short.

'I don't care if it's sacrilege – I'm not going to do it. Get that ?'

Joe joined Angus. He, too, preferred mutiny to murder. Torrence glared helplessly. The odds were against him and he was wise enough to know that the men would back Angus in any dispute. He could do no more than give in with bad grace. The party would stay in the *Red Glory* and let the enemy fire the first shot, if shots there must be.

'It's checkmate,' said Angus. 'Sen-Su will realize that mighty soon. Jamie tells me there are plenty of supplies aboard and they couldn't get us out for months. My only worry is that if they keep us cooped up here we shan't be able to find out what's happened to Davie and the others.'

All the men of the colony were called in for safety's sake. There was little over an hour of the short Asperian day remaining, and there was the risk of their being cut off by a party of Martians. Once or twice glimpses were caught of the little brown men on the escarpment of the further side, apparently bent on reconnaissance.

'Cooping up' seemed to be the programme, for when Torrence went to the entrance port with a rifle in his hands, the warning smack of a bullet on the steel side above him caused his hasty retreat. Angus grinned when he heard of it.

'Teaching the sniper a few tricks, are they ?' he said.

Night closed in without any further signs of activity. The port of the *Red Glory* was swung to and locked by old Jamie in the manner of one performing a ceremony. All sound of the outer world was shut away. The Martians could do what they liked: no portable weapon would be capable of making so much as a dent in the space ship's armour.

Angus awoke with a hand shaking his shoulder. He looked up to find Joe bending over him.

'Blast you, what's the matter ?' he mumbled sleepily.

'Looks like a deputation. Get your clothes on and come along.'

Dawn had just broken and from the windows of the living room they could observe three Martians who stood looking towards the ship. They had reached the beginning of the cleared pathway and were plainly ill at ease. The central figure upheld a stick to which was attached a piece of dirty, white rag. It was obviously intended for a sign of surrender. But why, Angus asked himself, should the Martians wish to surrender ? All three men had evidently suffered rough handling for their clothing was little more than a covering of tatters stained with blood. After a short consultation the two flanking men lifted their empty hands above their heads and all three advanced. Old Jamie hesitated a moment and then unlocked the port, beckoning to them to enter. The questioning he left to Angus who began with the monosyllable;

'Well ?'

The middle man, looking askance at several pistols trained upon him, lowered his flag of truce and answered with the characteristic lilt:

'We have come to surrender.'

Angus frowned. This was not his idea of Sen-Su's methods. 'And the rest of you ?' he asked.

'There are no more.' The Martian spoke slowly and with a depth of dejection.

'Talk sense. There were ninety-seven of you. Where are the rest ?'

'All gone. We were attacked. Great winged monsters which screamed fell on us out of the night. We shot at them and then we fought them hand to hand, but it was dark. There must have been thousands of them. We three got separated and they overlooked us or must have thought we were dead.'

'All the rest are dead ?'

The Martian shook a sorrowful head as though he considered the indignity greater than death.

'Only a few. The rest they took away. In the fight they seemed flimsy, but their wings are strong. They lifted our men, two to a man, and flew off with them. I don't think they took them far. We came to you because' – he hesitated uncertainly, uncomfortably – 'because you are our kind,' he finished abruptly.

Angus studied him hard, seemed satisfied, and nodded.

'We'll go and see your camp. Maybe we'll learn something there.'

Torrence demurred. 'It's a trap. They knew they couldn't touch us in here, so they're getting us into the open.'

Angus ignored him. The first officer's prestige had fallen to zero with the defeat of his sniping proposition. A dozen men, including old Jamie, set out to investigate.

The Martians had made a clearing for their camp, and when the Earthmen reached it they stopped to gasp aloud. The brown men had excelled themselves. It was the scene of an epic battle. Slaty, grey winged bodies strewed the place – literally hundreds had fallen in that fight. Not only was the ground a bloody shambles of hacked and twisted forms, but in the surrounding trees and bushes hung the corpses of those shot in mid-air. Lanky shapes, somehow unclean, their listless great wings stirring in the gentle breeze like patches of dirty sailcloth, while the steady drip-dripping of their crimson blood incarnadined the leaves below.

For some moments no one spoke. In Joe's mind arose the dim memory of old engravings depicting hell. Then Angus broke the silence.

'What a carnage. I've seen slaughter in my time, but this . . .'

The three Martians went forward and examined the dozen or more bodies of their men lying among those of the grey attackers. The wing talons had made them unpleasant sights.

'Sen-Su' asked Angus as they returned'

They shook their heads. The leader was not with his dead.

Angus threw back his head and looked speculatively up at the caves in the valley sides. Below one a glimmer of something bright caught his eyes. He pointed it out to Jamie, and the old man brought a pair of binoculars to bear.

'The buckle of a belt.' he said, 'a broad, Martian belt.'

Angus gave the order to return to the ship.

'You're not going after them ?' inquired Torrence.

'That's just what we damn well are.'

'But they're enemies and it's our duty –'

Angus stepped close to him.

'See here, you know too doggone much about duty. The Martians are human beings – they're our own kind. What's more, there are our own men to be found, too. If you think I'm going to stand by without reason while men of Earth, or Mars, are in the power of these repulsive spawn of miscegenation, you'd better think again. Get that ?'

Torrence wisely withdrew. Old Jamie proved reluctant to let them go, and sternly forbade any of his colonists to take part. He did his best to dissuade Angus though his manner showed that he had little hope of succeeding. Perhaps he spoke from a sense of duty, for when he found that the other was determined, he became lavish in his offers of weapons.

Rifles were discarded as unsuitable, but he insisted that each man should take several pistols since, in the unlikely event of success, the rescued must be armed. He pinned most faith to the long knives which would be invaluable for infighting. In addition, he insisted that all the available lamps be collected and affixed to the chests of the rescuers.

The *Red Glory* colonists collected to bid them farewell. There was a suspicion of envy in the eyes of some of the younger men, but Jamie's word remained law.

'Good luck, laddie, and God be with you,' said the old man to Angus.

He watched the twenty-seven from the *Argenta* and their three Martian companions with wistfulness as they scaled the valley wall. That was the spirit which had taken the Earth-men all over the system. Confidence that they could not lose the game. The last figure turned and waved a hand as it disappeared over the skyline. Old Jamie sighed. He wished he were young again, he'd show them – but he wasn't young. He was an old man, and getting sentimental.

He sighed again and turned back into the *Red Glory*.

IV

THE CAPTIVES

David awakened to a species of bedlam. He could hear Angus' shouting voice making a bass accompaniment to an unearthly screeching. He heard the other men jump up from sleep and leap into action. He started up with them, fumbling for the knife in its scabbard by his side. His hand was upon the hilt when long arms wrapped around him, pinning his own arms. He cried out. Dimly he could see furious activity taking place in the cave-mouth; dark shapes which jerked and fought. He struggled against the retaining arms aware only that this was an attack, by whom or what, he could not tell, though his mind jumped to the conclusion that the Martians were somewhere back of it.

He opened his mouth to call again, but before the cry came something was wrapped around his head. A dark sheet of unfamiliar substance which, by its feel, sent a surge of panic through his nerves. He lashed out as far as he could reach with his feet, but a moment later they were snatched from under him and secured by arms which seemed to wrap themselves more firmly about his legs than any human arms could hold. He wriggled, trying vainly to jerk off the grip. Through the shroud about his head he could still hear the sounds of turmoil, but they were swiftly growing fainter, and he could tell from the motions of his captors that he was being carried away.

At length the sounds dropped behind altogether, and the silence of their progress was broken only by soft footfalls and occasional, high pitched cadences from his bearers. He succeeded in twisting his head in the folds which covered it, and began to breathe more easily. With a faint hope, growing

38

ever fainter, he strained his ears in hope of pursuit. At last, hope died altogether. Perhaps all his companions had also been captured; perhaps they were dead; he did not know. He was only aware that all hope of rescue had gone.

For seeming hours the steady progress continued. At last his bearers seemed to find their method of transport inconvenient. They halted and set him on his feet. The arms about him remained inexorable, but the stifling cover was removed from his head. Thankfully he drew great breaths of fresh air, but he could see no more than before. The darkness was solid; unrelieved by the faintest glimmer. There came sounds of much movement near at hand. A few shrill notes such as he had heard before, and a grunt which might have come from a human throat. His heart bounded, and he decided to risk the return of the stifling cover.

'Hullo? Who's there?' he asked quietly.

An exclamation of surprise came out of the darkness.

'Cleary here. That's Robbins, isn't it?'

'Anyone else?'

There was no answer.

'I'm sure there were some others,' said the doctor's voice. 'But they're not here now,' he added a little unnecessarily.

'What are these things, and where are we?' said David.

'Lord knows what they are, but we're certainly somewhere inside Asperus.'

The captors continued to ignore their prisoners' talk. After a few minutes' rest they picked them up once more and continued their way through the darkness. This time progress was less uncomfortable, since there was no smothering cover.

'Do you know how many there are?' David inquired.

The doctor did not.

'If we could only see what they're like, I'd feel less uneasy,' he said.

They carried on a conversation in desultory phrases for some time. David had long ceased to struggle, and, as a result, his captor's hold had insensibly loosened. With the utmost caution he pressed his arms a little outward. His hand was already near his knife; with a little more play he might be able to snatch it out.

The ruse began to work. The arms did not tighten with suspicion, but eased a little to rid themselves of the strain.

39

David was beginning to extend his elbows further when the party came to a sudden stop.

From the darkness ahead came the click of something hard against metal, followed by a grating sound. Gates opening, David guessed. A moment later they stopped again and a similar series of sounds denoted another gate. Within a few minutes David began to see the first dim signs of reflected light on the wall where the tunnel turned, many yards ahead. He waited with a quickening excitement until he could see his captors. Two were carrying him, and, by turning his head, he could see two more dealing with the doctor. He took a deep breath and snatched for his knife.

The movement was a complete surprise. The first his bearers knew of it was that the blade was in his hand – it was almost the last they knew, for he cut at them savagely. Their screaming cries were deafening in the enclosed space. The hinder pair rashly dropped the doctor and hastened to their assistance. A second later he, too, was after them, knife in hand. David slashed wildly, dodging their raking claws and their attempts to entangle him in their wings. With the doctor's arrival in a rear attack, the fight was soon over. The two men, panting, faced one another over the four grey bodies.

'We must hide them quickly,' said David. 'Some more are bound to come along after all that row.'

Hastily they dragged the corpses into a small side passage and stood tensely listening. After a little while they relaxed. The grey creatures' cries, whether of alarm, or for help, appeared to have passed unnoticed. The problem now before them was one of direction. The way behind was out of the question, for it was barred by gates, and they faced the alternative of creeping along dark, narrow side passages or risking the lighted area ahead. In the end they elected for the latter; both had had enough of the darkness, and their enemies seemed unhindered by lack of light. The doctor adjusted his glasses which he had miraculously retained intact. He was a small man, inclined to stoutness and showing, in normal conditions, a cheery, rubicund face.

'Yes, towards the light, by all means,' he said.

He was aware of some slight professional regret that they could not spare time to examine the bodies of their late enemies, but he appreciated the necessity of getting clear.

They cautiously turned the corner ahead and found themselves facing a long vista of deserted tunnel lit at intervals by small, glowing lamps in the ceiling. There appeared to be no reason for this transition from darkness to light. David was aware of misgivings. This was the way their captors had been taking them, and it was obviously, for that reason, the way they should not go. However, if they should be attacked, they would have at least the advantage of seeing their attackers.

The walked on, every sense alert and their knives tightly clutched. To keep to the centre of the way seemed safest; one could not tell what might lurk in the small, unlighted side passages. Two hundred yards further they rounded a corner and abruptly debouched upon a still larger tunnel. Should they turn left or right? This new way, as dimly lit as the other, gave no clue. They were able to see perhaps fifty yards in each direction before turns cut off the view. David was about to speak when the doctor checked him. A faint sound had reached him from the left. Both peered in that direction, but its origin remained hidden by the corner. They drew back into the lesser tunnel to wait.

The approaching sound resolved into a steady trudge; the swish-swish of soft slippered feet upon the rock floor. David breathed more easily, for the monotonous walk could not be made by anyone seeking to investigate an alarm. The steps slowly continued to near the end of their passage. A figure which looked neither to left nor right, passed by. Both the watchers stared. They had expected one of the winged creatures, but –

'An Earthman,' gasped David.

The man caught his voice and turned towards them. He was elderly, and his head was but sparsely covered with grey hair. His face was pale and deeply graven with lines, but, for all its sorrow, it was kindly. Strapped upon his back he bore an enormous basket filled with broken ore. His expression changed to amazement as he saw them. He took an involuntary step in their direction and then stopped with doubt in his eyes. His attention seemed fastened more on their clothes than their faces.

'Who – who are you?' he asked in an unsteady voice.

David told him.

'You have come from "Outside"?' Something in his pronunciation of the last word seemed to imply inverted commas.

'We have,' admitted David, watching him closely, 'and we want to know how to get back?'

The old man slowly shook his head. A strange, musing look seemed to come over his face.

'There really is an "Outside"? Sometimes I think it was just all a dream.' He paused, looking at them with unseeing eyes. 'But no,' he added, 'it was no dream. A man could not dream a sight so lovely as a tree with the wind in its leaves, or the glory of the sun, any more than he could dream the curve of a wave.'

David and the doctor glanced at one another. The old man had forgotten their presence. He went on:

'Twenty-five years, oh God. Twenty-five years since I have seen those things.' The last word was a sob, and the tears ran unashamed down his cheeks. David took hold of his arm. He spoke gently.

'You don't understand. We want you to show us how to get out.'

The old man shook his head again.

'My boy, it is you who do not understand. – There is no getting out. Nobody has ever got out.'

'But –'

'Nobody, in twenty-five years.'

At the sight of their puzzled faces, he pulled himself together. The dreamy look vanished from his eyes and he spoke in a different voice.

'Come along with me, I'll explain.'

David relieved him of the basket and fixed it to his own, more able, shoulders. He was surprised to find it much lighter than it appeared, until he remembered the small size of Asperus.

The three walked together along the tunnel, crossed a hall which showed signs of being a natural cavern enlarged, and entered another tunnel. His name, said the old man, was John Fordham, and he began to relate the disastrous history of the *Red Glory*. He had, it appeared, been among the first to be taken prisoner. He was still talking when they reached another rock hall. In it a number of men and women were seated at long tables. All conversation ceased as they entered, and Fordham introduced them to the company:

'Two men from "Outside."'

The same look of suspicion that they had seen in Fordham's eyes appeared now upon every face, but, like his, it began to fade at the sight of the newcomers' clothing, as though their uniforms were assurances of identity. Both men and women present were clad in inadequate garments patched together from many pieces of coarse cloth. David estimated those present at one hundred and fifty, and subsequently that he was only seventeen short of the actual figure. Most of them were of middle, or later, middle age, with a sprinkling of the really elderly, and a very few younger members of approximately thirty or thirty-one. He noticed at a glance that women predominated.

With the lessening of suspicion they came crowding round, fingering the men's clothing as if it were something rare and precious, and asking innumerable questions. David slipped the basket of ore from his shoulders and dropped it on the floor. At his request for something to eat, bowls of fruit were immediately produced. The two attempted to answer the incessant questions as best they could. They described their own capture, but of conditions aboard the *Red Glory* they knew nothing. They could only say that Angus had sighted a wreck which might, or might not, be the *Red Glory*. At last the spate of questioning eased, and they had a chance to put their own perplexities forward. What were these creatures they called Batrachs? What was happening in this subterranean world? Was there really no possible means of escape?

Dr. Cleary was particularly exercised in the matter of the Batrachs. He had seen enough of them to form the opinion that they were mammals, but he was certain that no such forms had been found elsewhere in the system. He had a theory that similar systems produce similar forms, with, of course, adaptations to heat and gravitation, and he was fond of his theory. The presence of the Batrachs shook it severely.

Nobody was able to enlighten him. It was, it appeared, a subject never discussed with the Batrachs.

'You talk to them?' asked David incredulously.

'But of course – or, rather, they talk to us for we can imitate only a very few of their sounds. To get anything out of us, some of them had to learn our speech.'

They're not savages then?'

'Depends what you mean by a "savage." The Batrachs are highly intelligent in their own way, if that's what you want to know.'

'And your position is – ?'

43

VII

"WE'RE SLAVES – NOTHING MORE, NOR LESS"

David frowned in a puzzled fashion. He had just been told that the Batrachs numbered hundreds of thousands, if not millions. Surely it was not worth their while to enslave so few Earthmen. Several thousand slaves would have been understandable, but to maintain this handful of men and women couldn't even be economic. Ever since capture they had been confined beyond the double gates and all their food must be brought down from the surface. Their work could scarcely pay for the labour of feeding them. He put the point to Fordham who attempted to explain.

'As we told you, the Batrachs are intelligent, but their intelligence is difficult for them to apply. Perhaps you will find it easier to understand if I compare them with ourselves. Now, the first stepping stone of man's climb from savagery is really his opposed thumb. Don't misunderstand me, I know that there were lesser factors, and I don't forget that apes also have opposed thumbs, but the fact remains that without that useful tool, it is more than doubtful whether man could ever have risen as he has.

'Early man picked things up and played with them. He found in time, for instance, that if one stone were placed upon another, he could by standing on it, reach a fruit otherwise out of reach. He did not think the action out first; he did it by accident. and then took advantage of it. Once it had been done, his intelligence was stirred. and he could do it again. You see, this is the important point, his hands taught his mind in the beginning. The reasoning mind did not take real control until far later. If you doubt this, just consider how lazy people still try to make their hands teach their minds; they do it whenever they apply what we call a "hit and miss" method. So much for contrast.

'The Batrachs' intelligence, however, is fundamentally different. Their minds have not grown from actions. Somehow their mental evolution has progressed without the promptings of physical organs. The result is that they have reached a sticking point and they realize it. They can think, but they cannot *do*. They have no opposed thumb to help them. Control of their limbs is coarse compared with precision bequeathed to us by thousands of generations. Their talons have no more capability of fine accuracy than the claws of a tiger. They were – and are – in fact, in a very similar position to a paralysed man. Their only method of getting things done is to cause others to do them. And we,' he ended bitterly, 'have been those others.'

Cleary sat for some time in thought before he asked: 'But this vast system of caves? They're artificial. If your theory is right, they couldn't have dug them.'

'They might. It requires no great accuracy, and if you look you will see that all the work is rough and unmathematical in finish. But I suspect that there have been other captives before us. There are the gates. They are very old. Then, too, they have a few metal instruments – crude, of course, but certainly not made by the Batrachs themselves.'

The doctor whent on to ask more questions. The suggestion of the Batrachs' curious development interested him considerably. David's attention lapsed by degrees. He found his gaze wandering first over the rocky walls and bare utilities of this cave which, he understood, was the main living room of these lost Earthlings. From this he fell to examining the faces of those about him: tried to imagine what twenty-five years in such surroundings would mean, and failed. A sudden thought struck him. All these men and women had lived together for a quarter of a century . . .

'Are there no children?' he asked.

Even as the words left his lips, he realized that they were an indiscretion. A cold silence greeted the question. No one attempted an answer, and the eyes of all refused to meet his own. He had committed a dire solecism – touched a subject under strict taboo. It was queer – the condition of at least three of the women . . . He turned a bewildered face to the doctor. The little man shrugged his shoulders ever so tightly. Tactfully, he asked another question of John Fordham, and the awkward moment passed, though not without leaving a vestige of constraint.

Conversation was terminated by the sudden ringing of a bell. All present turned to face one of the tunnel mouths expectantly. After a wait of a few seconds, a figure strode out of it into the hall. Both men from the *Argenta* stared in surprise. They had expected the grey form of a Batrach, but the newcomer was a tall, well-built, young Earthman. His face, though clean cut, was pale and there was a sense of familiarity about it which David was at a loss to understand.

The men and women respectfully drew back, leaving a clear space down which he marched without a sideways glance until he reached a small, desk-like table at the head of the cavern. At it he seated himself to face the gathering, and in a hard, emotionless voice began to recite the names of those present. They had leisure to examine him more closely.

His age was around twenty-three, and he had the air of a man who performed a distasteful duty conscientiously. His clothing consisted of a knee-length tunic below which appeared trousers. Both garments were embroidered with patterns of geometrical design, as were the soft sandals on his feet. The roll-call completed, he paused a moment, then:

'John Fordham,' he said curtly.

The old man stepped forward. In a flash David saw the reason for the elusive familiarity of the young man's face. It was a youthful edition of the older man's. His son, perhaps? But there was no filial feeling in the curt voice.

'John Fordham, you have been reported to me as being one basket of iron ore short today. Why is this?'

The basket still lay where David had dropped it. As he made a movement to pick it up, the young man noticed him for the first time.

'Who are you?' There was the slightest flicker of surprise in his eyes as he scrutinized the pair. David hesitated and then explained, carefully omitting reference to the deaths of their captors.

'From "Outside"?'

Curious, David thought, this manner of treating the simple word 'outside'. The present emphasis on it was very different from the old man's.

'Yes,' he said.

'There has been a mistake. You should not have been brought here. You will follow me.'

They hesitated, but David's neighbour whispered:

46

'Go with him. He will take you through the gates and you will have a chance then. You've still got your knives.'

The young man took good care that his body should screen the combinations of the double gates as he worked them. The two with him noticed that they were leaving by a different route, for the tunnel was lighted and sloped steeply upwards.

In the walk of half a mile which followed. Cleary tried their guide with a number of questions which did not raise the success of even a monosyllabic reply. It was noticeable, also, that when they approached closely to him, the young man drew away with some ostentation. At length they began to meet or overtake others; men and women who had occasion to use one or other of the many side turnings. These, too, drew close to the walls as they passed, and more than once they saw noses wrinkled in distaste. The tunnel brought them at length to a hall.

The place was comparable in size with the cave in which the *Red Glory* survivors dwelt, but it was better lit, and better furnished. It even showed attempts at decoration by strictly geometric forms. But the greatest difference was that it was filled with the cheerful sounds of laughter and young voices. David felt a lightening of the load of depression which had crept over him. The doctor continued to wear a frown on his round face.

To complete the contrast with that other cave was the fact that every man or woman in sight was young, and many small children ran or crawled upon the floor, romping as freely and happily as any child born on Earth.

A pale cherub of four was playing near the entrance. David smiled at him and extended a friendly hand. The child looked up at the sound of his voice. One glance was enough; he gave a frightened howl and ran to bury his face in the tunic of a young woman nearby. The look David received from her dark eyes was murderous and loathing. She hastened away, comforting the frightened child.

David turned to the doctor in amazement. He felt slightly resentful; children, as a rule, liked him.

'What is it? What's wrong here?'

Cleary, still frowning, refused to commit himself.

'I don't know yet, but I've got an idea – just the glimmer of an idea.'

Their guide led out across the hall. As they approached the people shrank back to either side, the children ran whimpering to the women. Not a face in all the place, but expressed disgust. Twice they had to pause before groups which had not noticed their coming. Each time the young man called: 'Outside,' and the way cleared as though by magic. A queer fancy floated into David's mind – were not lepers in the East compelled to call 'Unclean' with much the same result?

They left the hall behind and still continued upward through the labyrinth. Now and then they had occasional sights of the grey forms of Batrachs going about their unknown business. Mostly they were on foot, but in the larger tunnels it was possible for them to fly, passing over the Earthmen with great swishes of their dry wings. The lighting grew dimmer as they proceeded and soon it became necessary for the guide to produce a lamp.

David began to toy with the idea of snatching the lamp and making a break for freedom. Surely, after all this climbing, they could not be far from the surface. He nudged Cleary and pointed suggestively to his knife. For some reason of his own the other shook his head. David let the matter drop and a few moments later, when the rays of the lamp fell upon another gate, was glad he had. It was opened like the others by a combination lock. The young man stood back for them to pass. The click of its fastening followed – but the man with the lamp was on the other side. Too late David realized what had happened. This was not another gate along the way, it was the door of a prison – and they, like fools, had walked straight into it. He drew his knife and sprang back, but the young man was safely out of reach. He turned away, paying no attention to David's threats, and soon his lamp became no more than a receding glow in the distance.

Darkness, intense and almost palpable, closed in. David shook the barred gate in futile fury, but he stopped abruptly at the sound of a movement in the blackness behind him.

'Who's there?' Mentally he cursed his voice for its unsteadiness; this dark was bad for a man's nerves.

A voice replied with a familiar, lilting tone.

'Good God, the Martians!' he cried.

48

VIII

ANGUS INVADES

Angus paused to muster his party at the cave-mouth.

'No talking!' he ordered, 'and step as lightly as possible. The brutes are nocturnal, and it's odds on we'll catch them sleeping now. Come on!'

He switched on the lamp upon his chest and led the way into the mountain. The entrance cave was much like the one in which they had been attacked. The dry, dusty floor sloped down towards the beginning of a narrower tunnel in which they could not walk more than two abreast.

They wound for fully half a mile of its evenly descending length before they came to the first forking of the way. Joe guessed that already they were below the level of the valley outside. Angus stopped and turned an investigating beam up each of the facing tunnels. Both were similar in size and in the degree of use they showed. One of the men picked out a slight obstruction on the smooth floor of the right hand path. He jumped forward and returned, displaying his find.

'A Martian boot,' said Angus, handling the soft leather. 'Somebody in that gang knows his stuff. Let's hope he's managed some more clues.'

The hope was fulfilled. They were subsequently assured that they were on the right track first by the discovery of the fellow boot, and, later, by the sight of a discarded cap. As yet they had had no sight of the Batrachs, and still the passages led down. Twice Joe, bringing up the rear, thought he heard a dry rustle behind him, but each time he swung his lamp, it revealed only the empty tunnel. They had now penetrated a long way into Asperus, and his suspicions were aroused.

'This is too easy to last,' he told himself uneasily.

A few minutes later, his fears were borne out. An unmistakable, murmurous swishing came from behind him. And, this time, the lamp showed a solid phalanx of grey, winged forms sweeping down in a rear attack. Almost without thought he drew his pistol and sent half a dozen shots crashing among them. Not a bullet could miss. They hesitated as several of their number fell, and swayed indecisively for a second. They rallied and came on, but their advance now was slow and deliberate. They appeared to have abandoned the notion of coming to grips.

Angus continued to lead his men steadily forward. Retreat was, for the present, cut off, but that had been almost inevitable in such catacombs. There was more pressing business to be attended to before they had to worry about the way back. Joe reloaded his piston and held it ready.

A turn of the passage brought them without warning into a large cave. The many black tunnel entrances dotting the walls on all sides suggested that it was a meeting place, a kind of public square of this subterranean world. By far its most disturbing feature was that in almost every entrance lurked grey, menacing figures. Angus grasped the danger at once. The Batrachs would have full room to use their wings and could attack from all sides simultaneously. Already not a few were taking to the air. The way behind was blocked. A swift glance showed that the tunnel directly opposite held no guard, and, at his command, the Earthmen made for it, crossing the wide floor in a series of leaps. To their surprise they reached it unattacked. The sense of uneasiness grew. The Batrachs followed at a distance.

'Don't like this,' muttered Angus. 'From what we've seen of them, they're fighters. I'll bet anything the blasted creatures have got something up their sleeves.'

Nevertheless, they continued unmolested for several hundred yards. Then, at a corner, Angus stopped dead. The way ahead was choked with Batrachs who stood blinking in the glare of the lights.

'Oho! So that's it. Sandwiching us, are they?' He settled a pistol in one hand and a knife in the other. 'Now for it!'

But still the Batrachs did not attack. There was a puzzled pause. Angus opened his mouth to speak, but before a word came, the floor gave way beneath him.

The next seconds were confusion. A writhing mass of men fell struggling sideways, swearing as they tried to disentangle themselves. Angus' pistol was knocked from his hand by the fall, but he staggered to his feet, still clutching the knife. The light on his chest remained unbroken, but it was obscured by the struggling bodies. The man next to him suddenly grabbed his arm. Angus tottered and lost his balance. He tripped over a prostrate form, and slid, head first, down a polished stone slope at prodigious speed. After a few breathtaking moments he sped from a kind of chute into a room crammed with the grey Batrachs.

The trap had been well planned. Half a dozen of them flung themselves upon him before he could rise. His knife arm was pinned to his side and despite all the extra power which the low gravitation gave him, he could not break their tenacious holds. Struggling and shrouded beneath the great wings, he could see little, but he was aware that others of his band were suffering a similar fate as they shot into the room. He could hear their muffled curses and grunts as they fought.

With a colossal heave he achieved a sitting position and struggled thence to his feet. The Batrachs still clung about him, pinioning his arms. By jerky, intermittent beams he could see all over the floor a series of struggling heaps with wings threshing furiously above as the men were secured and weighted down by numbers. He tried with all the force of desperation to wrench his right arm free, and bellowed futilely at his assailants:

'You lot of lousy sons of Satan. Just you wait till I get this knife free – I'll show you who's boss here. I'll carve your miserable, stringy carcasses into mincemeat, you –'

But the thin arms twined around him like ropes; not an inch did they give before all his violence. In the far corner he glimpsed Joe Seely rise for a moment, only to be dragged desperately down. The outlook was becoming ugly.

An interruption occured. A grey curtain on the opposite wall – made, he suspected from wing membrane – was twitched aside. In the doorway behind stood the short figure of Sen-Su. The Martian's clothes had been torn away, and the blood streamed down his brown skin from a dozen ragged cuts. In one hand he held a jagged ended metal bar. His expression was one of dismay until he saw Angus, upright, though helpless. His bullet head went down. He crouched, whirling the bar before him like a lethal flail, and launched forward in a mighty leap at the group which held the engineer. His crude weapon tore through the great wings as though they had been rotten cloth.

The Batrachs' thin bones snapped like sticks as his blows went home. The onslaught was more than they could stand; the hold on Angus loosened. They and others with them flung themselves upon the threshing demon, smothering him in their wings, twisting their long arms about him to bring him, still fighting, to the ground.

But Angus broke free. His long knife darted with a shimmer like lightning, slashing, thrusting, tearing about him. Those whom the blade touched sank to the floor; those whom it did not, backed from his neighbourhood. Chaos broke loose. The Batrachs holding other prisoners were trodden under the feet of their own kind in flight before Angus. Their grips slipped and the prone men snatched for their knives. Within a few seconds there were five at Angus' side, driving the grey ranks headlong with a line of slicing steel. The din of piercing cries increased as more and more men rose until all were on their feet. The surviving Batrachs fought each other to escape through the narrow doorway. A bellow of rage came from Angus. One of the escaping horde had hooked his sharp wing talon in the flesh of Sen-Su's shoulder and was dragging him away. Angus leapt in and slashed; slashed once and the wing was severed; slashed again and the head rolled away. He picked up Sen-Su and carried him aside. The Martian smiled faintly at his rescuer, then, swiftly, his expression changed. He pointed through the doorway.

'The others,' he cried. 'Quickly, before they get them away.'

Leaving a half dozen men to guard the few Batrach prisoners, Angus and the rest sped down the corridor. From somewhere ahead came the shrill sounds of Batrachs mingled with the confused babble of human voices. The next turn revealed winged figures fumbling frantically at the locks of barred gates set in side walls. They twisted around and emitted high cries as they saw the running men. One glance was enough to assure them that safety lay in flight. With mournful shrieks they disappeared into the blackness ahead.

A pistol made short work of the locks on the cell gates.

As the imprisoned Martians filed out, Angus caught sight of two familiar, lighter faces.

'David, Cleary,' he called. He greeted them excitedly and at once dragged the doctor off to have a look at Sen-Su's wounds.

'He's game,' he said. 'If he hadn't managed to break out of his cell and take a bit of the bars with him, we'd all be in cells by now.'

'Where are the rest?' he asked David as Cleary made his examination.

David looked puzzled.

'I mean the six men who were taken when you were.'

It was the first David had heard of them, and he said as much. Angus frowned.

'Then we'll have to go on – we can't leave the poor devils here.'

'There are more than those six,' said David. He told briefly of the *Red Glory* survivors and the others they had seen on the lower levels. Angus' frown grew still deeper as he listened. It was not a pleasant thought that Earthmen and women were existing here as slaves. He was at something of a loss to know how to proceed. Not only would it be difficult to find the way into these further tunnels, but there was no telling what further tricks the Batrachs might have in store.

'See if you can get anything out of the prisoners,' David suggested at length. 'They might be – er – persuaded to talk.'

Angus stared.

'You mean that they can talk? Those things?'

'I was told that some of them can – it's worth trying.'

One of the prisoners readily admitted to a knowledge of English. Was, in fact, fluent from long association with the slaves. His extremely high-pitched voice had a fraying effect on the nerves and he met with difficulties in the forms of labials, nevertheless, he was intelligible.

His information caused Angus to make a complete reassortment of ideas. Hitherto, he had considered the Batrachs as he would a species of wild animal – intelligent animals up to a point, but undisciplined; governed by no other instinct than that of the herd. But the view he was now given of them as a race under central authority, pulling together towards an ideal, killed all his preconceptions stone dead. He began to see, for instance, that the piles of dead on the site of the Martian camp represented not stupid ferocity, but determination and sacrifice. The Batrachs did not go into battle from sheer fighting instinct, but with a clear knowledge that many of their kind must fall for the eventual good of the race.

As one of his theories after another was tumbled down, it became clearer that he must take an entirely different course. He began to think of them as Bat-men, no longer as animals, a mental attitude which was the harder to adopt since hitherto no forms of life in the whole system had even competed intelligently with man. But there was one idea which underwent no readjustment – the Batrachs, whatever their status, must not be allowed to keep Earthmen and women as slaves.

Angus considered deeply.

With the rescued Martians and David and the doctor they numbered now one hundred and eight. Not a nugatory party, but certainly not formidable. In addition there was some shortage of arms and several men had been badly mauled. In continued skirmishes with groups of Batrachs their resistance would soon be worn down. Clearly a policy of guerilla warfare was unsuitable. He turned back to the prisoner.

'You talked about government. What form of government is this?'

Apparently there was an official council. The Batrach began to explain with some pride how it was formed. Angus cut him short.

'Take us to this council,' he ordered.

The Batrach agreed with an alacrity which caused him secret misgivings. He did his best to shake them off. After all, as he pointed out to David, whatever happened, it could scarcely make their position any worse.

IX

BEFORE THE COUNCIL

The Council Chamber, to which their guide led them, proved to be a cave of medium size, but sufficiently large to contain all the party. Word of their coming evidently preceded them, for they found a row of the creatures waiting; fifteen grey Batrachs who watched their arrival with calm, interested eyes. They sat upon a kind of stone shelf, seven to each side of one who was raised a little higher. It worried Angus a little that they showed no trace of fear, nor even anxiety, but, without delay, he plunged into the heart of the matter, addressing the central figure.

'We understand that you are holding a number of men and women of Earth prisoners here?'

The other studied Angus unhurriedly. When he answered, it was in a voice of lower pitch than their prisoner's, but still unpleasantly shrill.

'We are,' he said briefly.

'And we demand that you free them at once.'

'You "demand?" ' The Batrach showed a tinge of surprise at the choice of words. David and Joe exchanged glances. Both would have favoured a less outspoken policy. The party was scarcely in a position to 'demand' anything. But Angus merely nodded.

The Batrach forbore to point out that they were virtually prisoners themselves. He asked:

'And why do you think we would surrender prisoners to you who are useful to us?'

'Because you would stand a very poor chance of success against a warship from Earth.'

The Batrach considered.

'But if we imprison you, Earth may never know.'

There was an uneasy stir among most of the Martians and Earthmen present, but Angus smiled.

'That,' he said triumphantly, 'is where you are mistaken. You have held the passengers from the *Red Glory* only because we did not know what had become of them. We thought that the ship had been destroyed. Had we even suspected the true state of affairs, you would have had a visit from a warship long ago.

'Now, however, the case is altered. The *Argenta* is undamaged. If we fail to return, someone will take her back to Earth and report. Should you manage to prevent this, the delay will only be slight for our distination was known to officials at home and they will shortly send out a searching party.'

His words evidently went home to the council. They started to speak in their shrill, wailing tones. The central Batrach quieted them.

'It would mean the end for many of us,' he admitted, 'but I doubt even your people's power to conquer and hold all our passages and caves. It would, in fact, be better for them not to try. We could trap party after party so that they would starve. We know your weapons and we know their limitations.'

Angus shook his head.

'You know only a few of our weapons.' He went on to describe in some detail the effects of some poison gases, and to tell how the heavier types could be poured into the tunnel mouths to percolate throughout the Batrach warrens and kill any who got so much as a sniff of them.

55

Dissension followed. A few of the Batrachs took his statement for a fairy tale, others who had heard of gases from the slaves, knew better.

'But the prisoners – your own people – they would die too,' one objected.

Angus drew himself up.

'It is better,' he bluffed, 'for an Earthman to be dead than to be a slave. Our men would not wish to kill their own kind, but they would do it sooner than know that they lingered in servitude.'

He watched anxiously to see how this piece of heroics would be received. If it failed, he must change his tactics entirely. During the discussion which followed he kept his gaze level and steadfast. At length the spokesman addressed him again.

'We will agree to your demands. The survivors from the *Red Glory* shall go free.'

Angus allowed himself to relax slightly, but before he could reply, David was whispering in his ear.

'The others,' he was saying, 'the younger ones. Don't forget them.'

At the suggestion that these also were included in his demand, a great screeching of objections arose from the council. Again the spokesman quieted the rest with a wave of his winged arm.

'They are the children and the grandchildren of the others,' he said. 'We call them the New Generations. They have never been on the surface. They know only these caves which are their homes – it would not be kind to them to take them with you.'

Angus and his party stared. 'Would not be kind?' The effrontery of it. Would not be kind to take them into the sunlight – out of this gloomy labyrinth. He grew angry and his demands became eloquent. The Batrach listened patiently with a look in his eyes almost as though he were secretly amused. Once he began to break in with an objection. Angus swept on, brushing it aside unheard. At last he stopped. The spokesman, still with the disconcerting light in his eyes, hesitated and then gave in.

'We will agree not to stand in the way of their going.' he allowed.

56

Angus had won, but he was not easy. In the middle of his victory he was aware of a twinge of that same misgiving he had experienced earlier in the passages. Again it seemed too simple, and there was a something in the Batrach's tone . . .

The mixed party of Earthmen and Martians was conducted to a large cave to await the coming of the slaves. A few were jubilant and confident. Man, in their estimation had triumphed again, as man always would. But the majority was alert. Like Angus they felt that all was not so cut and dried as it appeared. There was a sense if not of treachery, at least of something very like it, in the air.

A group comprising Angus, David, Joe, Torrence, the doctor and Sen-Su – the latter bandaged, but not seriously hurt – stood apart from the rest, discussing the possibilities of the situation in undertones. Torrence was emphatically of the opinion that the Batrachs were not fetching the prisoners, but mustering for a mass attack with the intention of wiping out all in the cave.

Angus did not agree. For one thing he trusted the chief Batrach's word, and, for another, his threats of invasion from Earth had made a deep impression. All speculation was cut short by the arrival of a party of persons at the near end of the cave. One look showed David the people with whom he had recently talked.

'The *Red Glory* survivors,' he said.

The pitiful procession came slowly towards them. John Fordham walked a little ahead of the rest. There was no joy in his bearing; his feelings seemed too deep for that. He approached them, shuffling and tired, his shoulders bent as though they still supported his basket of ore. He looked at them with eyes which seemed to doubt what they saw. His voice quivered and broke as he asked:

'Is it true, what they told us ? Are we really going "Outside" ?'

'Yes,' Angus told him gently. 'It's quite true. We're taking you home.'

'Home.' The old man stood quite still. His arms hung slackly by his sides. His head went back as though he gazed beyond the rock about him, beyond the millions of miles of space, towards a swinging planet which was home. His breath caught in his throat. He buried his face in his hands and wept.

A woman came to David and plucked at his sleeve.

'And the children?' she asked in a low tone. 'The New Generation?'

'They're coming too,' he assured her.

She received the answer in silence. Drew a breath as though to speak. Shrugged her shoulders hopelessly and turned from him to join the others. There was no joy in her manner as she imparted the news. David almost followed her to ask questions, but remembered in time how his last question of the kind had been treated. He decided to wait for this puzzle to solve itself.

Up the far end of the cave another disturbance was occurring and he turned in company with the rest to discover that the New Generations were entering. Exclamations of surprise broke from both Earthmen and Martians as the stream of young men and women and children filed in. Nobody had thought to consider the probable number of the children and children's children.

Angus had guessed at a possible hundred or so. Suddenly confronted with more than five hundred, he stared with widening eyes. Even David and the doctor though somewhat prepared were taken aback. Cleary indulged in some hurried mental arithmetic.

The newcomers, accompanied by several Batrachs, remained crowded together at the end of the cave. Most kept their gazes averted, though a few examined Angus and his party with a kind of furtive interest. Their communal attitude was one of puzzled indecision. A short discussion resulted in one man detaching himself. As he approached, David recognized the firm step and fine carriage of their late guide. At a distance of two yards from the group he stopped short, scanning them with a look of distaste. He spoke in the tone of one accustomed to lead.

'You are from "Outside"?'

Again that curious treatment of the final word.

'We are,' Angus replied.

'What do you want here?'

Angus' eyebrows rose. This was scarcely the expected attitude of rescued towards rescuers.

'We have come to set you free.'

'Free?' The young man was puzzled. 'I don't understand you. We are free.'

There was a puzzled silence. Angus supplemented:

'We have a ship on which to take you, and your parents, back to your native planet – Earth.'

The young man continued to look mystified for a while. Then a thought appeared to strike him. With a look of growing, indignant horror in his eyes he asked:

'You want us to go "Outside"?'

'Of course,' said Angus curtly. He did not care for the young man's expression.

There was a muttering among the listening crowd of the New Generation. Partly nervous, but in greater part indignant. They shrank back towards the tunnel through which they had entered.

'Look,' whispered the doctor to David, pointing towards the group of original survivors. Most of the women were starting towards the New Generations with a complex expression. David analysed it as mingled yearning and hopelessness. He became aware that the groups of emotions in all parts of that cave fitted with none of his expectations.

'What is it?' he whispered back. 'I'm all at sea.'

Cleary shook his head.

'I think I'm getting it, but I'm not sure yet.

Meanwhile, on the young man's face, anger replaced consternation.

'How dare you make such a suggestion?' he demanded. 'No doubt you think that by those –' he pointed at Angus' weapons '– that you can force us. It may surprise you to know that you underrate us – we are not cowards. Get back to your filth. Get back to your "Outside". I am ashamed that our women have been allowed here to hear such an infamous, indecent suggestion. Had I known that they were to be exposed to such ignominy as this I would –'

Angus stepped forward, eyes narrowed. The young man recoiled; not from fear, but as though he avoided contamination. He turned round, addressing the crowd of the New Generation, already moving to the tunnel.

'Go!' he shouted. 'Go before the evil from outside can touch you.

He wheeled back to Angus. His countenance was a study in abhorrence, but he stood his ground, warding off the other from his people. Angus advanced slowly, bewildered. He put out his hand to press the other aside. The young man gave a cry of disgust, tore off the garment Angus had touched as though it were unclean, and hurled it from him. A loathsome reptile might have inspired the look which now dwelt in his eyes. A quick glance showed him that the last of his people were leaving. Without another word he turned and strode after them.

The silence of consternation held the cave. One voice rose at last to break it; John Fordham's.

'My son,' he cried. 'My son.'

But the retreating figure marched into the tunnel with never a backward glance.

X

THE POWER OF THE BATRACHS

Angus broke his trance of astonishment. Several of the *Red Glory* women had begun to sob desolately, hopelessly. He called Sen-Su to his side. Looking into his eyes he said:

'Sen-Su, can we work together?'

The Martian smiled slightly.

'Because I asked that question, they condemned me to exile. My whole faith has been that men should work together instead of exploiting one another.'

'And so they shall, by the Lord. We Earthmen have been a pack of fools – you've convinced me of that, Sen-Su. Henceforth, I'm with you Martians. When we get back to Earth –'

'But now we are still on Asperus,' Sen-Su pointed out. 'What do you wish me to do?'

'I want you to tell some of your men to take these *Red Glory* people to the surface, and to the ship. I'll send some of mine along too, to explain to old Jamie that it's on the level. Will they do that?'

Sen-Su nodded and turned to address his men in lilting Martian. A number of them crossed over and posted themselves beside the rescued.

'And the rest of us?' he inquired, turning back.

'The rest of us are going to get the New Generations out of this warren, whether they like it or not,' snapped Angus.

'You'll never do it,' Cleary prophesied quietly.

Angus glared.

'Who says?'

'I do. You don't know what you're up against.'

'I know that these damned Batrachs are holding them somehow.'

'I doubt it; I don't believe that the Batrachs could persuade them to go. They've been clever; they've hit mankind in his weakest spot. Damned clever.'

Angus shrugged his shoulders and went about directing the departure of the rest. The survivors at length trailed away, a weary, dejected lot. Some seemed half afraid to leave their prison. Twenty-five years is a long time, and their children had refused to go . . .

As the last of them disappeared a company of grey forms flew out of a large tunnel and up the cave. Angus' hand flew to his knife and then dropped as he recognized the Batrachs of the Council. The creatures alighted a few yards away and closed their wings. The leader advanced.

'They would not go?' he asked Angus.

'You knew damn well they wouldn't go. What I want to know is, why wouldn't they go? How did you stop them?'

'We did not stop them. They could have gone had they wished.'

'You did not hypnotize them? They were free?'

This time the Batrach really smiled.

'Freedom. How often have I heard the slaves speak of it?
– It is the obsession of your race. What is freedom?'

It occurred to Angus that this was not the simple question it sounded. He wrestled with it awkwardly:

'The power to do as you want.'

'Then the New Generations are indeed free.'

Angus gave it up. 'I don't believe you,' he said bluntly.

'Nevertheless, it is true. If you took the New Generations away by force – as perhaps you might – you would take them from happiness to misery.'

'I don't believe that, either. How can they be happy down here in these burrows?'

'You don't appreciate your own point. "Freedom is the power to do as you want." – Has it not occurred to you that the "want" might be suggested?'

Angus frowned. Someone else had spoken of suggestion. Yes,

Sen-Su had referred to it as one of the great forces. He looked at the Martian and saw comprehension dawning in his eyes.

'Come,' said the Batrach. 'Words won't convince you. I must show you why the New Generations will stay.'

He turned and led the way up an ascending passage. As he went he talked, giving them what was in effect an amplification of Fordham's explanation to David. The Batrachs, he reiterated, were making a great bid for the future of their race. They had knowledge, but they could not make even so simple a thing as a book to store that knowledge for the benefit of future generations. The Batrach held up his clumsy wing claw. What, he asked them, could be accomplished with so crude an instrument as that? They had tried always to educate the claw, but it was little use compared with even an uneducated hand with the advantage of the power to grip. They had been forced to turn to other methods.

'Just so, I am told,' he said, 'did your ancestors turn to the horse and to other animals to overcome some of their own limitations. Did you ever think of your horses as slaves?'

Doctor Cleary diverted the subject with a question.

'How did you Batrachs get here – there are no others that we know of in the system?'

'I can't tell you that,' the other admitted. 'There are legends, but they are vague. They tell of the Mother of all Batrachs, so great, so magnificent in her wings, that she could fly not merely as we fly, but out to the furthest stars in the sky. Now and again, however, even she tired and needed to rest, and on each world where she rested, she brought forth ten small Batrachs such as we. You can make what you like of that. It may be that the Mother was in reality, a space ship such as yours. I do not know. One thing is certain, and that is that we are admirably adapted to Asperus. We should be unable to fly on even the smallest of the major planets.'

'There is usually a basis of truth in such legends,' agreed the doctor. He was determined to protect as long as possible his theory of systematic species. He went on to question the other on his physical structure.

The rest of the men followed in silence as the two conversed. David and Joe felt little more than a curious interest in what the Batrach would reveal. Angus wore a puzzled frown. Torrence, as usual, was out of temper. He had abandoned the making of suggestions, but he knew what a man's attitude should be towards an inferior race. This meeting on an equal footing was, to him, not only improper, but weak. Sen-Su was paying close attention to the leading Batrach's talk, while the rest of the Council seemed to be content to bring up the rear.

At last came the glimmer of daylight far ahead. The Batrach led on without a pause. The doctor, watching him closely, saw that his eyes filmed over with a protective membrane as the light grew more intense. The passage rapidly broadened out until it became a wide cave with an extensive view over valleys and crags. On the rocky floor twenty or more children were playing with simple toys. In careful attendance lurked the figures of tall, grey, female Batrachs. Evidently this was the nursery of the grandchildren of the *Red Glory* survivors. David, mindful of his earlier experience, hung back, but Angus continued. A child noticed his coming and fled with a yelp of terror in the direction of the nearest Batrach. There was an indignant murmur from Torrence that the children were being taught to hate their own kind. He was surprised when the leader calmly nodded:

'But only those from "Outside",' the latter added.

'I don't see –' Angus began.

The Batrach checked him. 'Watch,' he said.

He indicated a small boy who was near the cave mouth. Outside, the sunlight was pouring down on a broad, smooth ledge. The contrasting world beyond seemed to intrigue the youngster. He was slowly edging towards the fascinating line of light. Once he looked back cautiously towards the other children and their attendants, but they gave no sign of noticing his manoeuvres. He crawled on to within six inches of the line of shadow and hesitated again. Finally he made up his mind and boldly stepped over. There was a sudden, ear-splitting crash from a metal gong. A breath of nauseating stench seemed to invade the cave. The child jumped back howling with terror. One of the female Batrachs swept forward and picked him up in a fold of her wing. He hid his face with its streaming tears in the comforting darkness it afforded.

'Behaviourism,' cried the doctor. 'A pure Behaviourist method.'

Angus' eyes were blazing with anger. He advanced upon the Batrach as though he would strike him.

'It's cruelty,' he shouted. 'Pure, wanton torture of these

children. I see it all now. You've brought up the New Generations to be so scared of you that they daren't do a thing you might resent. You had only to tell them that you wished them to stay, and they cringingly obeyed.'

Cleary intervened. 'Don't be a fool man. Did the leader, old Fordham's son cringe? Of course he didn't. He walked like a ruler. Besides, these children don't hate the Batrachs. Look there.'

The female Batrach, in a motherly way, had dispelled all the child's terror. He was clinging to her and almost laughing again. Angus and the others stared in bewilderment. There was no cruelty in the soft eyes with which she looked at the child – only concern that it should be happy once more. Torrence, in the background, muttered vengeful threats.

I'm damned if I get this,' Angus said. 'First she allows the child to be terrified out of its wits – then she's really worried when it is. What's it all for?'

'It's on the Behaviourist basis,' said the doctor, enthusiastically. 'A matter of conditioned reflexes.'

'That's all Greek to me.'

'You know what a reflex action is?'

'One that is instinctive.'

'Not quite that. One that takes place without conscious thought – not quite the same thing. An instinctive reaction is innate, but a reflex action is caused by subconscious memory.'

'That seems pretty much the same.'

'No it's not. Take our avoidance of fire. Very young children are attracted by the brightness of fire. They want to play with it – have no instinct to fear it. But you and I do not try to handle fire, in fact, we avoid coming into contact with it. But we don't say to ourselves each time, "This is fire – I must avoid it." The warning is subconscious – we "automatically" avoid it. In other words, sometime in the past we burned ourselves and stored up the subconscious memory that fire was painful.

'A conditioned reflex arose – it caused us to avoid anything in a condition of fire. It was the same with foods; some we "automatically" leave alone because we know they will make us ill. The same with all kinds of things. As a result we dislike even the smell or taste of them. Once you cut yourself on a sharp knife – now you "automatically" pick a knife up by the handle.'

'Then this . . . ?' asked Angus, indicating the children.

'All the children here will grow up hating the world out-side, and that hatred, properly fostered will become an inhibi-tion. They will not be able to leave these caves. The memory of that gong and the nauseating smell won't remain con-scious for long, but, if the treatment is continued (as, no doubt it is) the idea that "Outside" must be avoided will persist. From the behaviour of the adults it would appear most successful.'

'Do you mean to tell me that if I, as a child, had been treated in this way, I should hate the "Outside"?' demanded Angus.

'Certainly – why should you be different?'

'But – but I'm free. I can think for myself.'

'You think you can – but can you really? Every thought of yours is based on somebody's teaching, or a scrap of information picked up from somebody else. One might even say that there is no "you" – you are no more than a con-glomeration of bits of other people. It's true,' he added as Angus shook his head, 'think it over a bit. You are as much a product of conditions as these children will be.

'Given a completely uninstructed child, a blank canvas, so to speak, there is scarcely any code of belief, morals or behaviour which cannot be induced by careful training. You've only got to look at the violently differing codes upon Earth to see that.

'That's what the Batrach meant when he asked you what was freedom. We are always prompted or guided by others whether we like it, or not. Sen-Su said that suggestion was all powerful. He was right. This is its most subtle application.'

XI

THE ALTAR

There was a pause while all the men regarded the children in silence. The idea was slowly sinking into Angus' reluctant mind. Was it possible, he was wondering, to warp minds so that they saw nothing but horror in the fresh greenness of trees; so that the sun ceased to be the life giver, but became something indecent and fearful, never to be looked upon? It seemed impossible, and yet. . . .

David, too, was thinking. He remembered the decorations in the caves of the New Generations – not a natural form had been allowed to intrude. Every suggestion of the world 'Outside' had been rigidly excluded. He remembered, too, the expressions he had faced – hate, fear and disgust . . .

Torrence was not thinking. This foolery was taxing both his patience and his control. It was no mean task to keep his tongue still.

Again a child was approaching the line of sunlight. They watched in silence an exact repetition of the earlier episode.

'But why the gong?' asked Joe. 'Why not stop them each time?'

'That is simple,' the Batrach explained. 'Were we to stop them, they would resent it and end by disliking us – as it is, we comfort them after their fright and they love us for it.'

Joe's mouth opened wide. He had never considered the possibility of anyone loving a Batrach.

'Come,' the tall, grey figure added. 'I will show you one more piece of the life of the New Generations. I think it will convince you.'

He led the way back into the tunnel. The doctor hurried forward and walked abreast with him.

'Then you do not mind the *Red Glory* survivors leaving?' he asked.

'No. We could only get the coarsest of compulsory labour from them. It was their children we wanted. We had, at first,' he added, 'some difficulty in persuading them to bear.'

He went on to explain. The survivors' children had been taken from their parents as soon as possible and started on an elaborate course of conditioning to environment. Success had been immediate and the New Generation had been brought up thinking, feeling, acting and reacting in the ways the Batrachs wished – yet unaware of any compulsion. When the second generation began to appear it could be safely left with its parents save for regular periods of training in a nursery such as they had seen. The change was really very slight, he pointed out, none of the basic instincts was touched and character remained unaltered – only certain taboos became desirable, and certain desirables, taboo.

The doctor nodded thoughtfully.

'And so,' he said, 'our strongest point is our weakest.'

The Batrach was puzzled.

'I mean, our adaptability. It is that power which takes us into dry climates and wet tropics and polar regions, cold planets and hot planets, open spaces and confined quarters – has, in fact taken us all over the system. You have succeeded in turning that same adaptability to your own advantage.

'The others do not understand how the New Generations can be really happy in here, but I do. There never was (in this system, at least) a race so adaptable as we.'

The Batrach checked at last at a small doorway. Making a sign for silence, he led the way within.

They emerged upon a shelf partway up the wall of a large cavern. In the arrangement of the place there was more than a suggestion of the interior of a church. Row upon row the New Generations sat below them all gazing intently towards the far end at a feature which caused the Earthmen to stiffen with surprise. A long table stretched right across the cave and was covered by a cloth decorated with metal thread. The ornaments which rested upon it gave it the appearance of a kind of altar. Behind, outspread so that they covered most of the end wall, was a pair of wings patterned after those of the Batrachs. They had been skilfully fashioned from grey, lustrous metal which gleamed under an ingenious arrangement of the dim lights. Below them a man dressed in a grey tunic was in the act of mounting a few steps which led to a kind of rostrum.

He reached the platform and stood for a moment with his back to the audience gazing up at the great wings above him. Then he turned and began to speak in a calm, clear voice. His pale face was serious and there was no doubting the sincerity and strength of the belief which backed his words. But what words they were . . . The men's eyes grew wide as they listened.

'– Our ancestors sinned. They doubted, and doubt is sin. For that sin they were punished. They were cast into the nethermost "Outside" – a place of evil and terrors without names. They forfeited all; they had betrayed their faith and, as a punishment, their wings' – he dropped his voice as though grieving – 'were withered upon them. Shorter and shorter grew their arms, and less, generation by generation,

67

the spread of their wings until, at last, the membrane was gone and they were left as we are with but stunted growths.'

In a gesture he held out a pair of magnificent arms and stared at them.

'These,' he stretched them out towards the audience, 'these are the symbols of our fall; the badge of our shame.

'But,' – his voice rose triumphantly – 'through faith we shall win back. Beyond hope – damned through all eternity – are those "Outside". But our feet are already upon the road back. The Batrachs have taken us in and purified us. Here in the caverns of the chosen they have taken compassion upon us. We shall climb again to that high estate from which our ancestors fell.

'Slowly and surely we shall rise, scaling the firm rungs of faith. It will not come in our time, nor even in our children's time, for the return to grace is hard, but far, far in the future, men who have regained their lost wings – such wings as the Batrachs have – will look back upon us and praise us for our faith which paved the way. Therefore, I tell you, keep faith. Firm, steady and unfaltering faith so that a million yet to be born may one day look back and honour you. Imagine a man in the full glory of his restored wings who will whisper the name of one of you, saying: "She was my mother, and faith, my cradle." '

As the last words died away he turned to face again the huge, symbolic wings upon the wall. He raised his arms imploringly and stood motionless. There was not a sound to be heard in the cave.

On the ledge the men stood speechless, astounded by the travesty. There had been no bluffing. They caught the spirit of the men and women below. Intense, faithful, trusting, and, above all, convinced. That the Batrachs had taught this religion and the worship of the Wing, there could be no doubt – but that it had become a part of the worshippers' lives, there was equally little doubt. So simple.

A slightly new twist to the old Earth legend of angels, and there was the ideal, with the Batrachs already in the position of demi-gods.

David remembered old John Fordham's words – 'The Batrachs can think, but they cannot *do*.' He had been right. They had thought a new race of mankind into being, and this race, regarding them as saviours, would work for them

68

willingly and joyfully, secure in their faith. David's last hope died; the New Generations could never be rescued against such odds.

Torrence broke the silence with a shout. He swung himself over the edge of the rock shelf and dropped to the floor below. Before any could stop him he was on his feet and racing towards the far end. He leapt upon the rostrum and felled the speaker with a blow.

'Fools!' he shouted, swinging round on the startled audience. 'Fools! He lied to you. Nothing but lies. It's a plot of the Batrachs. Men never had wings – they never will have wings. They –'

'Blasphemer,' roared a voice. An echoing pandemonium broke loose, drowning Torrence's voice with its babel.

The audience rose to its feet. With murder in its eyes, it charged madly towards the rostrum.

Angus knew an infuriated mob when he saw one.

'My God, they'll lynch him,' he cried.

The Batrach beside him swooped down from the ledge and spread his wings; another followed his lead. Together they sped towards the lone figure of Torrence, at bay beneath the monstrous metal wings. Their talons snatched him up and lifted his struggling figure clear of the crowd just in time. A moment later they brought him back, pale and not a little scared, to the ledge. The Batrach, after a glance at the outraged worshippers on the floor below, led the way into the corridor. There, he turned and looked at them with eyes which held the faintest tinge of mockery.

'You are convinced?'

Angus nodded unhappily.

'You're devils, but you're clever devils.'

'And you will leave us in peace?'

'What else can we do?' Angus shrugged.

'You might gas us,' observed the Batrach with an inflection which called the bluff.

'All right. You win,' admitted Angus miserably.

'Goodbye,' said the Batrach.

As they took an uphill tunnel, Angus turned to the doctor.

'And you really think they're happy here?' he asked.

'Less unhappy than they'd be anywhere else,' was the reply, 'and what more can you wish any man?'

Sen-Su's lilting Martian voice joined in:

'And now ?'

'And now,' responded Angus. 'we go back to Earth to preach the brotherhood of man and the damnation of Batrachs.'

And so, though it is colonized, you will fail to find the word 'Asperus' on Earth's proud colonial lists.

The Mole Pirate

MURRAY LEINSTER

I

The story of the Mole Pirate properly begins neither with Jack Hill, who built the *Mole*, nor with Durran, who stole it and used it to acquire more loot and do more damage than any other pirate ever managed in an equal length of time.

The records begin with a Mrs. Frank P. Hohenstaufer, who appears only once in the entire affair, and with Professor Eisenstein who, whatever his prominence in history, vanishes with equal promptness from this tale.

Really, the career of Durran as the Mole Pirate was simply one long battle between himself, the scientist-criminal, and Jack Hill, the inventor we remember as the man who made the earth-plane possible. But the story does begin with Mrs. Hohenstaufer, however briefly she remains in it.

She was, it seems, washing dinner dishes on the screened-in back porch of her home in Wausakkee, New York. It was three o'clock in the afternoon of June 16, 1935. The sun was hot. The radio in the dining room droned through a news bulletin, amid sundry cracklings of summer static:

Police have found a hide-out they feel sure was used by James Durran, America's Public Enemy No. 1, for at least two weeks. Durran, formerly one of America's greatest scientists, has been living in the most squalid surroundings, amid great privation, since he made his cynical statement of his intention to renounce all ideas of morality and ethics for the so-called natural principle of living for one's own satisfaction only.

Durran's record to date shows that in six months he has

been the cause of eight deaths – two believed to be murders committed by him personally – and twelve robberies. His loot has totalled more than a hundred thousand dollars, but he lives in conditions of unbelievable squalidness.

Four members of his gang, recently captured, have been sentenced to life imprisonment and are now in Sing Sing prison—

Mrs. Frank P. Hohenstaufer dried dishes and meditated piously. It was good that the government required the broadcasters to emphasize the penalties dealt out to lawbreakers and not to talk about criminals until they were caught or nearly caught. It would make young men more law-abiding.

She looked complacently through the screening. The Albany highway soared past, not half a mile from her door. As she looked, a car slowed down and turned off to the county road. It disappeared from view behind a clump of trees.

Mrs. Hohenstaufer looked for it to reappear with a sensation of mild curiosity. But it did not. It remained hidden. For three, four, five minutes there was no sign of it. Then it showed again, sweeping back up on to the highway. Into low speed, racing in second – dodging two heavy trucks bound for Troy – and then into high, the car shot forward at its maximum speed until it became a dwindling speck in the distance.

Mrs. Hohenstaufer blinked. That was her clump of trees. These people, these tourists, had no respect for other people's property. Maybe they came to steal green stuff for a city apartment; maybe some of the tiny pines and cedars that city people were making a fad of just now.

Indignantly, Mrs. Hohenstaufer took off her apron. She marched the full half mile to the wood lot in the broiling sun, growing more indignant as she marched. She saw the tyre tracks of the car. It had crushed ruthlessly through the tender small growths which Mrs. Hohenstaufer expected to sell at the proper time for transplanting. She followed the tracks, growing more angry by the minute.

Then she saw a man lying on the ground. His sandy-brown whiskers and white hair looked vaguely familiar to her even at first glance, but then she grew horrified. He was bound hand and foot. He was quite unconscious, and blood flowed from a nasty blackjack wound on his temple. Mrs. Hohenstaufer squawked in dismay.

It was half an hour before the police came. In that time Mrs. Hohenstaufer had cut the ropes from about the man's body. She had carried him, herself, all the way back to the house. There she telephoned for the police and a doctor and regarded her patient with extreme disfavour. He was undoubtedly one of these criminals of whom the radio chattered constantly.

She greeted the police with indignant protests against their allowing criminals to clutter up the wood lots of law-abiding people with their victims and acquaintances.

Then the officers saw her patient.

'Good Heaven!' said the first. 'It's Professor Eisenstein! What the hell's happened to him?'

'Prof——' Mrs. Hohenstaufer squeaked. 'The scientist? The great scientist that all the papers print pictures of?'

'That's who,' said the cop. 'Here! We got to get him fixed up so he can tell us –'

The patient's eyes opened vaguely. His whiskers stirred. 'Durran,' said the injured man faintly, 'Durran, you *verdammt* fool, what is der idea?'

Then he looked bewildered.

The cops snapped phrases of explanation.

'An' you were talkin' about Durran,' said one of the two feverishly. 'Did he sock you, professor?'

'To be sure.' The white-haired man blinked and said angrily: 'I came out of my house and got in my car. I had an appointment to visit der American Electric laboratories, where Jack Hill is going to show off a most remarkable infention to-day. And halfway there, my chauffeur turned around, and he was not my chauffeur. He was Durran, whom I knew. And he hit me with a blackjack. I suppose he has stolen my car.'

'Right!' snapped the cop. 'Brady, you got it? Phone in an' give the alarm. Durran's in Professor Eisenstein's car, an' it's a blue Diessel, licence number is –'

The other cop snapped into the telephone. Plugs clicked. A smoothly running organization moved swiftly into action. Short radio waves carried a brisk, curt order into every police car in New York, and to police-car headquarters in at least two adjoining States. In fifteen minutes, by actual timing, there were more than two hundred police cars, at least a hundred traffic posts, and even a few stray members of the

73

general public feverishly on the lookout for Professor Eisenstein's blue Diessel, because it contained America's Public Enemy No. 1.

And all that effort and all that searching was in vain. Because the blue Diessel was parked outside the American Electric laboratories, where Professor Eisenstein had an appointment, and nobody thought of noticing it.

It was not until Professor Eisenstein's secretary was notified of his whereabouts and telephoned an apologetic message to the laboratory that the blue Diesel was noticed. The professor and Mrs. Hohenstaufer immediately vanished from the tale of the Mole Pirate. But in the meantime things had happened.

II

Jack Hill was talking to reporters in the machine-shop section of the American Electric laboratories. The lathes and machine tools were covered over, for the moment, and there were a dozen or more of folding chairs in view. On the table before Jack there was a large sheet of white-painted metal, on which stood a block of brass and a small but intricate contrivance of radio tubes and the like. Behind him a wide curtain hid the farther wall.

'I'll give you a part of the idea now,' said Jack. 'Professor Eisenstein is late, but I don't want to start the apparatus until he gets here.'

'What's all this performance about, anyway?' demanded a man from the *Mirror*. 'Somebody said you had some kind of gadget that made you able to walk through walls.'

'I'd hate to tell you what I can do,' returned Jack. 'You wouldn't believe me. I'd rather show you. I've been experimenting on a rather neglected aspect of the atom. You know, of course, that the atom is regarded to-day as a sort of miniature solar system, a nucleus like a sun with a greater or lesser number of electrons revolving around it like planets?'

'Yeah.' The *Mirror* man had appointed himself spokesman. 'We know all that stuff.'

'Good!' said Jack. 'Then we can talk about magnets first. In ordinary iron the molecules have north and south poles,

74

like all other molecules, but they point in every possible direction, helter-skelter. They have magnetism in them, but it isn't organized. Pointing haphazard, though each one is a miniature magnet, in the mass they neutralize each other. It's only when the whole mass of iron is magnetized that all the poles point in the same direction – or only when they all point in the same direction that it's magnetized. Is that clear, too?'

'Yeah! I hadda do an interview with Eisenstein once,' said the *Mirror* man. 'He said I had a brain for that stuff.'

'Kind of him,' observed Jack. 'Now I've been trying to carry the idea of organization a bit further. Not only molecules but atoms have poles, and they point helter-skelter in every direction, too. Suppose I got them all to point in one direction. What would happen then?'

'You could walk through walls?' hazarded the *Mirror* man.

Jack grinned. 'Not so fast! Let's think it over first. An atom is a miniature solar system. That means it's practically flat. But with such flatnesses pointing in every direction – well, an enlarged picture of any sort of matter would be just about like a dozen packs of cards being poured from one basket to another and back again. They'd be fluttering every which way. You couldn't swing a stick through those falling cards without hitting a lot of them.'

'Not unless you were pretty good,' conceded the *Mirror* man.

'But if you had the same number of cards falling, only in a neat and orderly fashion, every one parallel, so they'd stack up all face down in the bottom basket – It's a standard card trick to spring a pack of cards from one hand to the other like that. You could swing a stick through that bunch.'

'You might knock one of 'em away,' said the *Mirror* man cautiously, 'but you wouldn't mess up the whole works. They wouldn't block up the whole distance between the baskets.'

'Just so!' said Jack approvingly. 'Professor Eisenstein was right. You do have a head for this stuff. Now the object of my experiments has been to arrange the atoms in a solid object like the second bunch of cards. They're flat. And it turns out that when they're arranged that way, all parallel, they block so small a proportion of the space they ordinarily close up, that they will pass right through ordinary matter with only the slightest of resistance. And that resistance comes from just such accidental collisions as you suggested.'

There was a stirring at the door. The snow-white hair and bushy, sandy whiskers of Professor Eisenstein came into the room. He beamed at Jack and the reporters. He spoke separately to Gail Kennedy, bending over her hand. The girl looked at him queerly. She was here because she intended to marry Jack and wanted to share in this triumph.

Her father and half the higher-ups of American Electric came in after the professor. Gail's face stiffened when her father's eyes fell upon her. He did not approve of Jack Hill.

'*Ach*, my young friend!' said Professor Eisenstein blandly.

A flash bulb flared as he shook hands with Jack. A news photographer changed plates in his camera and abstractly envisioned the caption. It would be 'Eisenstein Congratulates Youthful American Scientist', if this demonstration came out all right, and 'Eisenstein Condoles' if it didn't.

'You go on with your explanation,' said Eisenstein cordially. 'I sit at your feet and listen. Presently I make an announcement which will surprise eferybody.'

He sat down benignly. Gail looked at him, at her father, and back to Eisenstein. A moment later she appeared to be puzzled and uneasy. Her eyes remained on Eisenstein.

'I had just explained to these gentlemen,' said Jack, 'the object of my experimenting, the co-ordination of atom poles and what might be expected to result. I think all of you are familiar with the reasoning, since there's been a good deal of controversy about it. It was suggested that any co-ordinated matter would collapse into something like neutronium. Fortunately, it doesn't.'

He flung a switch and vacuum tubes glowed. A curious, ghostly light appeared above the white-painted sheet of metal on the table.

'The field of force,' he explained, 'which arranges the atoms in any substance so that they all point the same way.'

He switched off the tubes. The light died. He picked up the block of brass that was on the table. He placed it where the light had been.

'I am going to co-ordinate all the atom poles in this piece of brass,' he observed. 'Around the shop, here, the men say that a thing treated in this way is dematerialized. Watch!'

76

He flung the switch again and as the eerie white light flared on, the solid mass of brass seemed to glow of itself. Its surfaces ceased to reflect a brazen colour. They emitted the ghostly hue of the field light. Then it seemed that the block glowed within. The light seemed to come from inside the block as well as from its outer edge.

The whole thing took place in only the part of a second. A swift, smooth, soundless glowing of the block, which began at the outside and seemed to move inward – and cease. Then there was nothing visible at all but the queer glow itself.

Jack turned off the field. The light vanished. But the metal block did not spring back into view. Instead of a solid cube of polished brass there was the tenuous, misty outline of a cube. It looked unsubstantial, fragile. It looked like the ghost of a block of metal.

'It's still there,' said Jack, 'but you're looking past the edges of the atoms, so it's very nearly transparent. It's just as solid, in its way, as it ever was. It weighs as much. It conducts electricity just as well. But it's in a state that isn't usual in nature, just as megnetism isn't usual. The poles of its atoms all point the same way. Now look!'

He swept his hand through the misty block. He lighted a match and held it in the middle of the phantom. It burned, where Jack had claimed there was solid brass. A sceptical silence hung among the reporters.

Then the *Mirror* man said: 'That's a good trick, but if it wasn't phony –'

'What?'

'If that brass were still there, an' it would pass through anything else, it'd slide right through that sheet metal an' drop through the floor!'

'Radioactivity,' said Jack. 'The only exception. When co-ordinated matter is bombarded by radioactive particles, some of the atoms are knocked halfway back to normal. This paint has thorium oxide in it and it's slightly radioactive. Come here a moment.'

The *Mirror* man went sceptically forward. He suddenly reached out and passed his hands through the phantom block.

'It's a phony!' he said firmly. You're trying' to put somethin' over on us!'

'Put on these gloves,' said Jack. 'They've been painted with more of the same radioactive paint.'

The *Mirror* man incredulously obeyed. He reached again for the phantom block. And he gasped. Because his hands, encased in these gloves, touched something which was not only solid, but heavy. He picked it up, held it high, and his face was a study in stupefaction and unwilling belief. He staggered over to the nearest of his confrères.

'By cripes!' he said dazedly. 'It is real, even if you can't see it! Put y'hands on it!'

The other reporter, who was seated at the table, put his hands right through the object he could very dimly see. And to the *Mirror* man the brass block was solid. It was heavy. He gasped again and his hold relaxed. The phantom slipped from his fingers.

'Look out!'

The man gasped for the third time as the phantom object dropped. And it looked so utterly unsubstantial that the eye denied its weight. It should have floated down like gossamer, or so it seemed. But it did fall with the forthrightness of something very heavy indeed.

The man who had just put his hand through it now instinctively held them out to catch it. He cupped them, in anticipation of something very fragile and light. The phantom struck his hands. It went through them, and he could not feel it. It reached his knees and penetrated them. It dropped to the floor and through it, and did not as much as stir the cloth of the seated man's trousers.

'That's gone,' said Jack dryly, 'though I intended to reverse the process and bring it back to normal. It's falling down toward the centre of the earth, now, encountering just about as much resistance from earth and stone as if it were falling through air. I don't think any of us are likely to see it again.'

Professor Eisenstein beamed. The *Mirror* man put his head in his hands. The other reporters babbled together. Gail Kennedy looked frequently and uneasily at Professor Eisenstein. A telephone rang stridently somewhere. Somebody answered it, out of sight.

'Have I gone nuts?' the *Mirror* man exclaimed.

'I don't think so,' Jack assured him. 'If you have, all the rest of us will be nuts, too, in just a moment. Because what I've showed you is just a preparation for this.'

He turned and pushed aside a curtain. It took nearly a

minute to clear the thing behind it, because the curtain hid a space all of forty feet long, and most of that space was filled with an altogether-extraordinary object.

While Jack thrust at the curtain a distant voice said, evidently into a telephone: 'Professor Eisenstein's secretary? Yes, the prof –'

Noise cut out the rest of it. Gail Kennedy looked puzzledly at Professor Eisenstein. He was abruptly alert and feral. He was listening. His eyes, which had been benign, became quite otherwise. And Gail Kennedy suddenly looked as if she could not believe a thought which had come to her and which she could not dismiss. She stared at Professor Eisenstein in something approaching horror.

Jack turned again to his audience. He had cleared the *Mole* to view. It was a vessel of riveted steel plates quite ten yards in length and about three yards high. There was a rough approximation to torpedo shape, but the likeness was not carried far enough to keep it from looking more like a military tank than anything else.

Yet even that wasn't a fair description. There were neither tractor treads nor wheels. Instead, there was a marine screw propeller in the back and four others mounted vertically where wheels should have been. They made the *Mole* into something it was quite impossible to classify.

It was plainly designed for travel, but in what medium was not clear. It did not seem fitted for travel in any medium at all. Yet the heavy glass windows and a carefully curved and fitted door which opened inward seemed to imply that the medium was one in which a supply of air for breathing would need to be carried along.

'Here's the ship,' said Jack curtly. 'In it the field of force I just generated is made use of. There's a generator of that field inside the ship, also a means of alternating the gradually weakening field to restore it to its normal condition. The process is the same as demagnetization.

'I go inside the ship. I start the motors, and these screws try to revolve. They can't. I turn on the force field and the ship becomes like that block of brass. It tries to drop down to the centre of the earth as that block of brass did. But the screws revolve, then. And they are coated with a film of radioactive matter somewhat thinner than the paint on this sheet of metal. It's not radioactive enough to keep them "solid". It's just enough so that they seem to work in a medium about like – like –'

'Mashed potatoes,' put in Professor Eisenstein unexpectedly. 'Much better than water for der screws to work in.'

'Just so,' agreed Jack. 'And now, to save a lot of talk, I'll show you how it works.'

He opened the curved door.

Professor Eisenstein got up and said blandly: 'May I come? I haff der most implicit confidence.'

Jack stared. Then he said gratefully: 'Thanks! Of course you can come'. To the others he added: 'I'll put the ship through the same process as the block of brass, only I'll rematerialize it. Please don't stand where I'm going to bring it back. The results would be very unpleasant.'

He ushered the white-haired scientist into the door. Gail Kennedy stood up and opened her mouth, her features queerly twisted. But before she could speak Jack was inside the *Mole* and the door had closed behind him.

There was a queer roaring noise out-of-doors. It sounded like the popping of many motorcycles. But those in the machine shop of the American Electric Co. paid no heed. They were giving strict and exclusive attention to the ungainly metal shape before them.

Something rumbled inside it. The screws stirred. Then a ghostly eerie light seemed to envelop it. And in the fraction of a second the solid mass of metal shimmered into insubstantiality. It was transparent – more transparent than any glass. Only its outline could be seen, ghostly and improbable.

The screws, for an instant, seemed somehow more solid than the rest. They swept swiftly into motion, into a blur which was like the most airy of froth. The whole ship settled with a speed which suggested falling, until those screws took hold – in the solid concrete of the floor.

It was a phantom, then, which remained steady for an instant. Then the tail propeller began to revolve. And slowly, slowly, the apparition, the ghost, the utterly unreal outline, began to move. The tail propeller swept through the concrete of the floor. The whole thing moved forward with a quick gathering of speed which was exactly like a ship getting under way. It reached the wall it went through it. And not one brick, not one grain of mortar, was disturbed.

Stunned silence. Then a startled babbling.

A news photographer wailed: 'I didn't flash it! I didn't flash it!'

And then there was a sudden rush of figures at the doors – dark blue-clad figures with service revolvers out and ready.

'Where's the man who calls himself Professor Eisenstein?' barked a police lieutenant, staring around. 'We want him!'

The president of American Electric, no less, stood up indignantly. 'What's all this about?' he demanded furiously. 'What the devil –'

'Durran!' snapped the cop. 'He knocked Professor Eisenstein on the head an hour ago. Stole his car. One of your men here said Professor Eisenstein was right in here. That must be Durran himself! Where is he?'

Then Gail Kennedy gave a little choked cry. And as she uttered the cry the shimmering, ghostly outline of the *Mole* rose up through the floor. Somebody leaped to be away from it. It went to the end of the room and out through the wall beyond. And again there was not a brick or a grain of mortar disturbed.

'He's – in that!' said Gail, her throat constricted. 'With Jack! Hide! You policemen! Hide, quickly!'

And for long minutes there was incoherent argument with the police before the ghostly *Mole* appeared again. Its pointed beak came through the wall to the right. It was a wraith. It was unreal. It was not substance, as we know substance. It came, slowing as it came, and checked itself by a reversal of its tail propeller. It was still, a hair-raising spectacle to the policemen who had not been prepared for such a sight.

And suddenly an eerie light seemed to envelop it and fade, and its substance thickened and thickened. Its vertical screws, revolving freely in the concrete, found resistance to their movement. They climbed upward, lifting the whole *Mole*.

And then, as the eerie light grew very faint and died, the *Mole* became actually solid. It became real, and it was a massive construction of riveted steel plates, unlike anything else that had ever existed on earth. Its solidity came as a shock. The clang of its door as it opened broke a silence of almost superstitious intensity.

Jack Hill came out. 'As you see.' he said quietly, 'it works.'

Gail darted forward to him, clutching him convulsively. 'Jack!' she gasped. 'Professor Eisenstein! He's Durran! I thought he'd kill you and take the *Mole* –'

Then a bland voice came from the open door of the earthship. 'In that case, I can drop both my accent and my whiskers.'

The man who had been taken for Eisenstein tugged at his face. The identifying sandy whiskers came off. He flung away the white wig. He grinned at the men in the machine shop.

'As Professor Eisenstein,' he said amusedly, 'I promised an announcement that would surprise everybody; I make it now. I'm Durran.'

A pistol barked savagely. He jerked backward and almost closed the door. Through the remaining crack he said more amusedly still:

'I add that my mission here to-day was much more successful than I expected. I hoped to gain useful information. I've got something much better, this contrivance and instruction in its use gained on a trial trip. Au'voir!'

The door slammed. Almost instantly a fusillade of shots poured upon the machine. But the eerie white light enveloped it. It shimmered into a phantom which fell with a jerk. Then the vertical screws caught it again and raised it back into view. It did not come all the way above the surface of the ground, now. Only half its bulk appeared above the surface. Only the tip of the phantom tail screw appeared above the concrete in which it suddenly began to revolve with a quite impossible freedom. It moved forward – through the wall. It vanished.

'And I showed him all about the thing!' said Jack Hill. 'I even let him steer it!'

There were policemen outside the laboratory. Durran was America's Public Enemy No. 1. When a force of uniformed men swarmed inside the laboratory, another force took position outside, to surround him in case he evaded the others momentarily. These men outside saw what looked like the ghost of a prehistoric monster swimming across solid ground toward them. Superstitious terror afflicted some. Others did not believe their eyes. But a hoarse and raging voice from the laboratory shouted for them to shoot it.

They did. Their bullets went through it without affecting it in the least. It was not substance of a sort that bullets could harm. But as if they were annoying, like pin pricks, the phantom dived. It sank out of sight in the solid earth underfoot, still moving forward. Some of the policemen thought they could feel a slight vibration, as if of engines underground.

III

Durran vanished in and with the *Mole* at something after four o'clock. At five, a motorist drove shakenly to the home of his family physician. His nerves were badly frayed.

He had seen something like a turtle, he said, swimming in the solid earth. It was larger than his car, and it swam across a concrete road, in the concrete, directly before him. It was a ghost, and there were no ghosts. His nerves were upset, and he wanted treatment which would keep him from seeing anything like that again.

At five thirty, a motorist stopped at a filling station for gas and heard screams coming from inside it. The proprietor was dead on the floor, shot. A coloured helper was having hysterics beside his body.

The helper told what ought to have been a wholly improbable story of a monstrous engine which appeared out of thin air, from which a man emerged and shot the filling-station proprietor. He then took gas and lubricating oil, got back inside the monstrous thing of steel plates, and it melted into thin air again and its ghost swam away.

These two stories were accidents. Durran's real intentions began to be outlined later on – at eight o'clock, to be exact.

At that time – eight o'clock, p.m. Eastern Daylight Saving Time of June 16th – there were extra editions of practically all newspapers on the streets, screaming in headlines of Durran's latest exploit. 'Durran Steals Mystery Invention.' 'Durran Escapes Under Fire.' 'Durran Scores On Cops Again.' 'Scientist-Criminal Turns Phantom.'

But on the whole, the theft of the *Mole* was played down. The story of what the *Mole* could do was too improbable to go in a news story. It was held over for the Sunday editions, when feature writers could take space to expound it – if it were still true.

Most of the papers did not really believe in the *Mole*, despite the impassioned assertions of the reporters who had been on the spot. And in a thousand police stations the official report of Durran's latest exploit and the contrivance he now had at his disposal were subjects for argument. Mostly, the report was regarded with extreme scepticism.

More than one inquiry came to the originating office of that report, demanding confirmation. And more than one hard-headed police official did not bother to inquire, but indignantly reported that a hoax was being put over by somebody. The New York State Police – and half of them, even, did not quite believe it – were spending as much effort trying to get the facts accepted as they were in trying to devise some method of coping with the menace the *Mole* now represented.

But none of this uncertainty and none of this indignation was to be found in the Wedgewood Arsenal, in Connecticut. Durran simply wasn't thought of there. It was a semi-Federal, semi-State, arsenal which did not manufacture arms. It was a storage place with a stout captain of regulars assigned to duty in it, and a small detail of soldiers who served practically as watchmen. It was an emergency depot of weapons and ammunition, and the duty of its official caretaker was mainly that of making out documents in triplicate for some purpose unknown.

In that arsenal, at eight p.m., there was peace. The captain in charge was seated at a desk in a corner of the vast hall which had once been used for indoor close-order drill by a National Guard organization. He was making out a document in triplicate. His pen scratched. He smoked languidly on a fat cigar. From time to time he mopped his forehead, because it was hot.

There was utter quietness, utter peace. It was so still that it seemed even the scratching of the captain's pen aroused murmurous echoes. The captain sighed heavily. His chair squeaked. That did arouse echoes, which rang about the huge hall for seconds before they died away reluctantly.

Then there was another sound – the very ghost of a sound. Something impalpable and tenuous rose out of the floor. First a round snout, which was quite transparent. After it a mis-shapen huge bulk, all of thirty feet long.

The whole thing was unsubstantial, was unreal. It came to a stop in the middle of the vast open space. It flared brightly and the glare against the walls made the captain start. He whirled in his chair. Then his eyes widened. His mouth dropped open.

The light was fading, and as it faded the ghost in the middle of the ex-armoury grew solid. Noises came from it, which became louder and more real. Then the light died away completely and there was a huge thing of entirely substantial steel plates at rest. Huge steel screws beneath it turned for a space, and wooden planks splintered and cracked. Then all was still.

Dazedly, blankly, like an automaton, the army captain got up and walked stiffly toward the thing that had appeared before him. Perhaps he had some wild thought of visitors from another world or another dimension. As a curved steel door clanked open he went rigid. But the figure which stepped out was a man, a tall man with a merciless sort of amusement on his face. He brought up a pistol. He fired it, quite ruthlessly and quite coolly.

The explosion echoed thunderously. It made a drum roll of sound as the echoes played about between the walls and among the rafters. The captain choked and made absurd motions with his hands. He collapsed on the floor.

Then the man from the solidified phantom set to work, very coolly and very swiftly.

When a corporal of the guard detail came in anxiously some few minutes later, he saw a shimmering something sinking through the floor. He thought it was an optical illusion. It made his hair stand on end for an instant, but he forgot it when he saw his commanding officer lying dead on the floor.

He, and the other men of the guard, and later on the local police, too, found no sign of any way by which an assassin could have got into the arsenal. They found the captain stretched on the floor with a bullet in his heart and an expression of blank amazement on his face.

They found a case of loaded hand grenades gone, several light machine guns missing, with drums of ammunition for them, and an assortment of tear gas and a few lethal gas bombs. Also a certain amount of engineers' stores had been taken, notably blocks of compressed guncotton intended to be used for demolition purposes.

IV

Sing Sing prison is forty miles from the Wedgewood Arsenal, and the *Mole* turned up there at eleven o'clock. Its speed was greater than that performance would indicate, however, and it is probable that Durran stopped somewhere to rest and possibly to investigate the *Mole's* various mechanisms more thoroughly.

It is clear that he had made his plans in detail between four in the afternoon, when he stole the *Mole*, and eight at night when he raided the arsenal. To carry out his plans he needed help, and he knew where to get it, and he had to move fast to avoid being outguessed and having his men hidden away from him.

It was a bright, moonlit night. At eleven o'clock the high concrete walls of the prison glowed palely where the moonlight struck them and showed utterly black in shadow. White arc lights glittered within the prison enclosure, making a misty white aura above the walls. The cell blocks of course were dark, save where corridors reached to windows and showed the faint illumination within. The lights of Ossining twinkled in the distance, and a river steamer floated upstream out in the middle of the Hudson River.

A guard, pacing the top of the wall, saw a vaguely moving thing outside. It was too dark for him to see it clearly, but he watched curiously. Something was moving, past question, but the suspicion of Sing Sing guards is directed always toward the interior, not the outside, of the prison.

The guard could make out only motion. Its line was clear. The guard fixed his eyes upon a whitish stone on the ground and waited for it to be obscured. The moving thing, whatever it was, went smoothly up to that stone. The guard watched.

But the movement continued and it was past the whitish stone, and the stone was not hidden for even an instant. The guard grew doubtful and even more curious. The inexplicable thing was headed straight for the base of the wall. He saw or felt it reach a spot directly below him. Movement continued. Then there wasn't anything there at all. He called to the guard next to him.

'Somethin' funny,' he said uneasily. 'I saw somethin' movin', down on the ground, an' then it wasn't there.'

The other guard looked down, but on the inside of the wall, because it is toward the inside that a prison guard bends all his alertness. He searched with his eyes.

'There it is!'

He pointed. From the height of the wall and in the glare of the bright arc lights a misty, phantomlike shape could be seen. But it could be looked through. The floor of the exercise yard was visible below it.

'What the hell!' said the second guard.

'Y'guess we oughta make a report? It looks like a ghost!'

The second guard continued to stare. The phantom swam smoothly across the open space. It reached the outer wall of a cell block. It vanished, apparently into that wall.

'Gosh!' said the second guard. 'That was a funny thing!'

'What was it? A ghost?'

'Hell, no!' said the second guard, without conviction. 'It was some mist, maybe. A speck of fog or somethin'. Y'want to be kidded to death?'

The first guard did not want to be kidded to death. He returned to his pacing back and forth.

Quietness again. A steamer out of sight on the river hooted dismally. Somewhere a motor car hummed along a distant road. Insects stridulated insistently. The crunch of feet on concrete. The wailing, plaintive cry of some night bird. One minute, two, five, ten minutes, with only such sounds as guards upon a tall concrete wall will normally hear.

Then a single, muted '*pop*' in a cell block. A small sound, but distinctive. Every guard in every watching post heard it and gripped his rifle more tightly. Every man turned to face the sound. Silence. Another muted '*pop*'. Then the sudden snarling roar of a machine gun, unmistakable even though it came from a cell block.

An instant later, there was the shattering concussion of a hand grenade. Glass in the cell block broke out and went tinkling down the stone sides of the building. A neat row of windows gaped glassless into the night. Then a man screamed, a high, shrill scream that was not less horrible from being distant. Another shattering explosion. Yet another.

Guards raced for the building. Then pandemonium broke loose. The guards on the wall stayed there. It was their job to check a break, if one came, on the outer defences. But they saw running men with rifles make for the cell block. They heard shouts, yells, howlings of terror and of exultation alike. The cell building became a madhouse.

And then a series of detonations began which were

thunderous in intensity and deliberate in spacing, suggesting an inhumanly cold-blooded destructiveness at work. After each explosion came screams.

Then the men on the wall saw a phantom come out of the cell building. It was feet above the level of the exercise yard. It was unsubstantial and unreal. It was the wraith of a nightmare.

Shimmering, ghostly, impossible, it careened out of the wall and toppled to the ground. It seemed to bury itself – if a ghost can bury itself – before it came slowly into view again.

Not one shot was fired at it. It was impossible. It was a figment of the imagination. It simply could not be.

The phantom swam across the exercise yard of Sing Sing prison. It moved steadily toward the massive, monstrous outer wall of the prison. It reached that wall. It went into it. It vanished.

The guard who had first sensed movement outside now looked down again, shivering a little. He would not have known what the phantom of the *Mole* was, even if he could have seen it clearly.

But he saw nothing. He did sense that something was moving down on the ground below him, but that was all. A vague stirring moved soundlessly away from the prison walls and vanished into darkness. He did not shoot at it because he saw nothing to shoot at.

That was his story after the whole disturbance was ended, and he stuck to it. He wasn't believed, of course. There were four prisoners missing, twenty or thirty injured by explosions, three guards dead and others hurt, and nearly one floor of the northeast cell block so badly wrecked as practically to be destroyed. A guard who said he saw something moving, but nothing to shoot at, was not telling a plausible story. Four men, escaping, should have made a magnificent target in the arc-lighted exercise yard.

It was not until the next day that a reasonable two was put to an incredible two and an inevitable four was arrived at. The missing prisoners were pals of Durran's. The phantom seen by the guards, the explosives, the destruction told –

Taken with the raid on the Wedgewood Arsenal, the uproar at Sing Sing made it perfectly clear that Durran, in the *Mole*, was a criminal with an unparalleled opportunity to gratify his every impulse. And it seemed likely that he intended to use his opportunity.

For the next three days there was no word of Durran or the *Mole* or any of the four men he had raided Sing Sing to release.

Something had been pieced together of what he did, of course. On the 17th, a radio store in Newburgh, New York, was looted of practically all its material for radio repairs, wire, tubes, sockets, transformers, batteries – everything that goes into the making of a radio receiver was stolen. That same night, too, fancy groceries in considerable quantity were taken from the town's most expensive food shop.

Next day, on the 18th, police surveillance of the women formerly beloved by the released prisoners came to an abrupt end. The women vanished. From sheer habit the police instituted the customary search to find out who had taken them away from their usual haunts. They discovered nothing.

It is reasonable to assume that the first two thefts, of radio parts and food, were preparatory moves by Durran. The removal of the women was a part of the process of making the released prisoners contented.

Meanwhile Durran seems to have used all his intelligence in the examination of the *Mole*, and on the 19th he was probably busy. Certainly on the 20th he was prepared for action on a larger scale than before.

At nine thirty that night a thunderous, clanging uproar broke out in Newburgh. The outdoor alarm gong of the First National Bank went off with a tremendous noise. Simultaneously, the local police station received due warning of prowlers at work inside the bank. It was not a large bank, but even the little ones have more than one burglar-alarm system installed nowadays.

In less than five minutes from the sounding of the alarm, a patrol load of cops was on hand, prepared to do battle with bank robbers. The bank doors were closed and locked. They were opened from inside by a scared and bewildered watchman. He had heard the gongs, too. His own telltale registered a disturbance. But he could find no sign of anything wrong.

Then bank officials tore up in a motor car. A third alarm system had reported disturbance to the home of the cashier. They crowded into the bank, to be faced by puzzled cops and nearly deafened by the insistent, frantic clanging of the alarm gong outside.

Somebody managed to turn off the gong. It looked as if a freak accident had set off every protective device at once. The cops were rather sheepish, standing embattled in the bank with absolutely nothing to do. But there could be nothing wrong.

The vault was closed and locked and obviously untouched. There were no thieves to rout, it seemed, so the question became that of discovering and correcting the flaw in all the protective devices. The bank suddenly gleamed light everywhere. A master switch turned on every light in the place.

Then they saw the *Mole*. It was quite stationary. It was a huge, shimmering phantom, its bow end lost in the metal of the vault. Its tail, also, vanished into the side wall of the bank building. Standing still as it was, it could be examined with some detail, and presently it was observed that the four huge, vertical screws turned lazily, maintaining its position in spite of the gravity pull which tried to drag it down to the centre of the earth.

Men shot at it. The bullets went harmlessly through. They hacked at it with fire axes from a case on the wall. The blows spent themselves on seemingly empty air. The men drew back, regarding the earth-ship helplessly. Then a minor official of the bank, desperately daring, plunged first his hand and then his whole body into the phantom.

He could feel no resistance to his movements. The *Mole* remained as transparent and as unsubstantial as before. But, from within, he could see wraiths about him – machinery like gossamer, even men, like ghosts.

One of those ghosts saw him and pointed at him. Another ghost rocked back and forth, laughing, and the bank clerk was tormented by the suspicion that he heard a whispering thread of that Homeric laughter. Then one of the ghosts made an elaborate, mocking gesture of lifting a phantom cap in greeting.

A roar of rage brought the clerk out of the phantom. Somebody had thought to put his ear to the vault. And there was movement within. Through the steel walls came thumpings, crashings, bumps. There were men at work within the monstrous sealed safe – methodical bangings, deliberate, purposeful thuds and clanks.

'They're looting it!' panted the president of the bank,

purple with rage. 'Looting it! And the time lock's on, and we can't get in!'

Something like a dozen armed policemen and half a dozen bank officials stood helplessly by, hearing the sounds from within the vault. They went on for half an hour. Then the *Mole* backed comfortably out of the vault wall, a ghost in being, went through the side wall of the bank, and swam off into the utter unreachability of its peculiar state of existence.

When the time locks permitted the vault to be opened, the worst fears of the bank's officers were realized. The contents of the vault had been leisurely sorted over. Currency, negotiable bonds, the contents of the safe-deposit boxes – everything was gone. And the furnishings of the vault were wreckage.

They went to Jack Hill next morning and found him haggard from four days and nights of work to cope with the catastrophe whose ultimate possibilities he foresaw. He was in the machine shop of the American Electronic laboratories again.

Gail Kennedy was with him, trying to persuade him to stop and rest. The visitors were an impressive lot. Police officials, banking potentates, and representatives of liability insurance companies. They regarded Jack with profound hostility.

'Mr. Hill,' said an eminent banker, in a voice that quivered with indignation, 'I suppose you realize what you have done?'

'Thoroughly!'

'Now what are you going to do about it? Every bank in the country is at the mercy of this Durran, through the hellish contrivance you made. No man's property is safe.'

'Rather more important,' observed Jack, 'no man's life is safe, either, if Durran wants to kill him.'

'But how can this menace, this pirate, be handled?' Again the eminent banker spoke. As if of old habit, his voice took on an oratorical intonation. 'When the arsenals of our government furnish him with explosives, our prisons with men, and the devil with ideas –'

'Oh, it's bad,' said Jack. 'It's very bad. But I'm working now to stop it. I'd like to know if he's changed the *Mole* about any, though. What's he done?'

They told him about the Newburgh robbery – more than fifty thousand dollars in currency gone, the contents of the safe deposit boxes –

'That doesn't help me!' insisted Jack. 'The *Mole* is pretty big. As I built it, that robbery would have been impossible. It couldn't be materialized inside a bank vault. There'd be no room.'

So far they'd told him only the results of the robbery. Now they told him the details of their helplessness while it went on.

Jack nodded in satisfaction. 'I see! He's improved the ship. But for those screws you saw revolve, the *Mole* would drop straight through the earth to its centre, as a block of brass did here. And, of course, if a man stepped out of the *Mole* while it was dematerialized, he'd drop too, without some device to hold him up.'

There were protests that men had been heard at work inside the vault.

'I know,' agreed Jack. 'But they weren't phantoms! Durran has fitted up an extra force-field apparatus. He can materialize a part of the *Mole* without materializing the whole. He drove the ship so its bow stuck out into clear space inside the vault. Then he materialized that part, and that part only.

'There were a couple of men in it. They got out, gathered up their loot, and stored it in that part of the ship, and then Durran dematerialized that part again so that it was like the rest of the ship. And then he swam away.'

'But what can we do to stop this – this ghastly performance? demanded the banker agitatedly. 'He can rob any bank in the country! He can steal any treasure, any security, any record!'

'You can hide your treasures,' replied Jack meditatively. 'Until he starts kidnapping people and forcing them to tell where valuables are, he'll be stopped. And – well – the screws of the ship are coated with a thin film of thorium alloy. That is partly real in both states of existence. You can make bullets and bombs of radioactive substances. Anything that's radioactive will find the *Mole* substantial. You can puncture it with radioactive bullets or shatter it with bomb fragments, if they happen to be radioactive, too.'

'You suggest,' said the banker in almost hysterical indignation, 'that we shoot Durran with radium bullets? Think of the cost!'

'It's more important to think of results, just now,' said Jack dryly. 'But thorium will do instead of radium, and that isn't too expensive to use in gas mantles. It'll be cheap enough.

'I have, though, one really comforting thing to tell you. The *Mole* was built for underground exploration, to find veins of mineral and for geological study generally. It isn't designed for the use to which Durran is putting it.

'And the entire resources of American Electric are now put into the building of a new *Mole* which will be designed for offensive warfare underground. As soon as our new ship is complete – and it should not be long, working as we are – we'll find the original *Mole* and destroy it.'

Gail Kennedy said something to him in a low tone.

Jack nodded wearily. 'Something to keep Durran from materializing his ship even in part? Why, yes! My head's tired, Gail. I should have thought of that.'

He turned to the others. 'I have one promising suggestion, due to Miss Kennedy. I've proved that two solid bodies can occupy the same space at the same time. But they can't, in the same state. If there is any matter more solid than air where the *Mole* materializes, the sudden appearance of extra material in the same space will cause an explosion. So you can stack bars of iron, and grilles, and string wires inside your vaults. Make it impossible for any part of the *Mole* big enough to hold a man and loot to materialize without including some such extra matter. If Durran tries, he'll blow up the *Mole*! It's worth trying, anyhow.'

He passed his hand wearily over his forehead when the indignation party went out of the laboratory. Gail smiled anxiously up at him.

'I was stupid,' said Jack tiredly. 'I guess you're right, Gail. The new ship is taking form very nicely. The others can carry on without me. And my head's so tired I'll do better work if I rest.'

Jack took a last look at the partly completed ship that was to take the place of the *Mole*, in the very spot where the *Mole* had been. There was a great deal yet to be done to this new ship, but to Jack it already looked promising. He saw past the incomplete framing, the only partly assembled machinery. He visualized the streamlined vessel of the new design, more heavily powered than the *Mole*.

Its sustaining screws worked on swivels and at full speed would not only sustain but help to propel it. And there was armament. A two-pounder gun with a spotter searchlight. When this ship was dematerialized, it would fire shells that would be utterly unsubstantial to anything but the *Mole* or radioactive minerals.

The spotter searchlight would emit extraordinarily polarized light, capable of penetrating stone and rock in the state of matter Jack had discovered. This ship should have no trouble overtaking and destroying the *Mole*.

'Funny,' said Jack suddenly. 'I never thought of it before. This ship's going to be fast. And we could build faster ones yet. Planes, in fact. Earth-planes! They'd carry passengers. No storms. No wind currents. Earth-plane ports in the centre of our biggest cities. Climb in an earth-plane and fly through the earth's core, beneath or through mountains and oceans. And they'd be fast!'

Gail smiled at him. 'Good! You think about that instead of Durran for a while. But I'm going to take you home and make you go to sleep.'

She did take him home. She made him promise to rest at once. But, tired as he was, this new vision of a medium in which the commerce of the world would be carried on in the future, kept him awake for a long time.

It seemed that Jack had just dropped off to sleep when the strident ringing of a telephone beside his bed got him heavily awake. He glanced at a clock. It was after midnight – one o'clock. He picked up the phone.

'Hello?'

'Mr. Hill!' panted a voice at the other end of the wire. 'This's the gate watchman at the lab. There's all hell loose inside! Explosions! I sent for the cops, but it sounds like Durran's back! Listen!'

Over the wire came dull concussions. Then the extraordinarily distinct sound of running feet, a slamming door. A voice panted, and Jack caught the message before the watchman repeated it:

'The *Mole*'s in there an' Durran is flinging bombs outta a tube in front. They turn to real as they come out. He's blown the new *Mole* to hell an' he's smashin' the lab!'

A terrific detonation seemed almost to smash the telephone instrument at the other end of the wire.

It was stupidity, of course, that caused the destruction of the American Electric experimental laboratories. Durran made a thorough job of it. It seems that he stopped at a construction job in Schenectady and looted the powder house of explosives to have plenty for his purpose. And it is quite certain how he came to know of the need to blow up the laboratory.

Within an hour after Jack had reassured the committee of bankers and police officials, the newspapers had the whole story. To Jack the need of secrecy was so self evident that he had not thought of mentioning it. But to a banker the self evident necessity was to reassure the public so there would be no runs on banks.

To police officials the self evident necessity was to make a public statement meaning that they had a clue and an arrest would follow shortly. To the newspapers and the broadcasters there was no thought of anything but hot news, to be passed on at once.

In consequence, Jack's assurance and his description of a ship being built to hunt down and destroy the *Mole* was given to the whole world. And with the world it went to Durran, too.

He acted immediately. He destroyed the laboratory where the Nemesis of the *Mole* was preparing. And he did more. When Jack got to the scene of the disaster, fire roared among the ruins. The new ship was scrap iron. And plans, apparatus, formulas, everything the laboratories had contained, were gone.

Gail ran up to him as he surveyed the wreckage. 'I'm so sorry, Jack!'

'It is pretty,' returned Jack sardonically. 'Those damned fools had to tip Durran to everything! And he'll be on the lookout now. My guess is that he'll try to bump me off, because with everything in the lab in flames, I'm the only one with all the stuff in my head to make another *Mole* possible. We've got to start building another one in secrecy. Better, half a dozen of them. He won't be able to destroy all of them before one's finished.'

Gail's father came up, scowling. 'This costs American Electric better than a million,' he said bitterly.

'Ill give it back to you,' said Jack harshly. 'Listen to me!'

Swiftly, tersely, he talked of a new transportation system which would be faster and safer than any the world had ever known before, and wholly independent of weather or storms.

'And if that doesn't make up for the damage,' he added savagely, 'here's another: We dig shafts for mines, now. We send men down underground. But Durran's found a way to materialise a part of the *Mole* while leaving the rest a phantom. If he can do that, so can we, and the other way about too.

'Why can't we lower a tank with a field of force in it? Dematerialize it and lower it through rock and stone to an ore bed as deep as we want to go – ten miles if necessary? Then turn on the field force to dematerialize the ore that's inside that tank.

'The ore, being made phantom to the rest of the world, will be actual to the tank. And we can haul tank and ore up to the surface as easily as they'd drop to the centre of the earth. Once above ground we rematerialize both.'

Kennedy stared. Then his eyes flared triumphantly. 'That does it! You win, Jack! No matter how much damage Durran does, that one trick pays for it and more besides.'

Then Gail Kennedy screamed. A ghostly something – eerie and unbelievable in the red firelight – moved toward them.

'The *Mole*!'

In one instant Jack had Gail up in his arms. He sprinted – toward the *Mole*. He had seen a curious ring of solidity, upheld in mid-air, silhouetted against the blazing laboratory. And that would be the tube he'd heard about, through which bombs were dropped to become 'real' as they emerged.

Jack plunged past that bomb tube and the ghostly *Mole*. Once past. Durran would have to turn the earth-ship to bring the tube to bear, and that would take time. In a straightaway pursuit it could run him down on foot. But now it –

A hand grenade went off behind him. Earth spattered him. Something stung his leg, numbing it. Warm stuff flowed down it. Then he was at a car. He flung Gail inside, jammed on the starter, and jerked it into first. The phantom of the *Mole* was turning. It came toward him again. And he shot away at forty-five miles an hour which became fifty and then sixty as he got on to a clear straight road.

'You father,' said Jack coolly, as he pushed the car to a higher speed yet, 'may think I'm a coward. But Durran has destroyed nearly or quite every record of how the *Mole* was built. I'm the only man who can build another force-field generator without those destroyed drawings and figures. I simply have to save that knowledge until I can get it down on paper.'

Then Gail said in a rather choked voice: 'I'm – wondering about my father.'

For answer, Jack swung right, left, right again. He drew to a stop before a drug store. He called the gate watchman at the laboratory from the phone booth. In seconds, Gail was talking to her father.

'He says you did the right thing,' she reported an instant later. 'Durran did intent to get you. But – my father thinks that if he saw that you picked me up, he may think that the best way to handle you is to be able to threaten me. So I'm forbidden to go home. Dad's going to get a fast car and meet us. He's going to send me away. You, too, most likely. You're important.'

Jack grunted. 'Where do we meet your father ?' he demanded. When she told him, he swung the car and headed that way.

They were three hundred miles away by dawn, and Jack flung himself headlong into the tedious, exacting work of drafting new plans from memory, building a new force-field generator also from memory, and of necessity for its construction determining all over again the constants needed for the calculation of certain of its parts.

He barely took time to eat and sleep, but in seven days he was ready to install new force-field generators as fast as they could be built in the new and faster earth-ships already taking shape in a dozen widely separated machine shops.

Three of those days were taken up by the need to repeat work already done, the results of which had been destroyed with the American Electric laboratory.

During that week, however, Durran progressed from the status of front-page news to a point where he was practically all the news there was. For one day after the American Electric fire, there was no report of his activity anywhere.

No authentic report, that is. A hysterical public reported the presence of the *Mole* from something like one hundred and fifty different points within a three-hundred-mile radius of its last appearance, and declared Durran busy at crimes ranging from the setting of forest fires and wholesale kidnappings to the robbery of a chicken coop in East Orange, New Jersey.

Actually Durran was still trying to reach and kill Jack Hill, as his solitary dangerous opponent. He had materialized a part of the *Mole* in the cellar of the house next to Jack's home. He hoped that Jack would return to his home, if only momentarily, to secure personal possessions or records. With the *Mole* part phantom and part real in the cellar of the house next door, his followers seized and bound and gagged the occupants of that house and watched comfortably for Jack's return.

He did not appear, though Durran waited for him for twelve hours. At the end of that time he took on board the men who had been watching, dematerialized the *Mole*, and moved away. But he left an incendiary bomb under Jack's house, and the firemen who vainly fought the blaze it started discovered the helplessness and the sufferings of the people next door.

Then the *Mole* began its career – the part for which it is remembered, at any rate. At dawn it was sighted in Troy, crawling deliberately out of a national bank building. A policeman shot at it and blew his whistle frantically. It swam indifferently for two blocks along the trolley tracks of Troy's main street.

While twenty police made frantic, helpless gestures, it crawled into another bank. It remained there for half an hour, its blunt nose thrust through the solid metal of a vault and its sustaining screws turning lazily. Then it sank abruptly into the ground. Its exit from town was unobserved. Both banks were looted.

At nine o'clock the Merchants' National Bank in Albany was open for business. There were a few more than the normal number of customers inside. The *Mole* swam through the walls and came into view. A stenographer saw it and screamed. There was a sudden glow of eerie whitish light at its snout.

A round ring of solid matter appeared, incredibly floating in mid-air at the forefront of a monster which seemed made of the most tenuous of fog. Something hard and round and quite solid dribbled out of that ring. It fell to the floor and exploded into a blinding haze of tear gas. More flares of eerie whitish light. More solidity appeared. Men got out and worked swiftly.

Police charged in from the street and were met by machine-gun fire. A hand grenade followed. The list of dead and injured was horrifying. Presently the *Mole* swam deliberately out into the street. It passed through a trolley-car, in which women fainted. It turned into the town's greatest jewellery store. Another tear-gas bomb. Ten minutes, and it came out again. Crowds swarmed about the scene of excitement. The *Mole* insolently moved upon and through the helpless police.

And in Albany Durran or one of his men committed a wholly causeless atrocity. A hand grenade dropped from the solidifying ring where the crowd was thickest. There was no reason or excuse for it. The hospitals of Albany were crowded with injured, alike those directly mangled by the grenade and in the panic which followed its explosion.

The *Mole* went on, insolently and deliberately looting bank after bank before the eyes of the police. There was no defence against it. Treasure locked in the bank vaults was but made more convenient for Durran's men. Left elsewhere, they drove out or blinded would-be defenders with tear-gas and machine-gun fire, with hand grenades always in reserve.

The *Mole* stayed two hours and a half in Albany. Its loot was something over three-quarters of a million dollars.

It reached Poughkeepsie at dusk. But here it was expected. A radium paint concern supplied the police with radioactive material. Daubed on bullets, the paint did all that Jack Hill had promised. A storm of paint-smeared lead poured upon the misty monster at its first sighting. Direct hits, instead of going harmlessly through a phantom, seemed to encounter resistance. Some punctured the nearly invisible steel plates when fired at sufficiently close range. Glancing hits – glanced. Several police were injured by ricochets.

The *Mole* dived at the first sign of injury. In seconds its shimmering, unreal rounded back was sinking into the pavement, which stopped what bullets seemed to penetrate rather than pass harmlessly through its impalpable armour. Rather quaintly, too, the painted bullets seemed likely to be effective in an unexpected way.

Once having punctured the *Mole's* hull, it was of course as difficult for them to get out as to get in. And they were 'real' in both the actual world and the strange universe of the *Mole*. They caught at once in the pavement and the hull and prevented the *Mole* from sinking out of sight. For minutes, the *Mole* seemed to be held fast. Then a terrific explosion underground flung up the street. A second, a third.

Otherwise unable to escape, Durran had materialized high explosives in the solid earth and set them off. He blasted away the roadway in which the bullets were caught. They undoubtedly remained inside the hull, but when no longer held fast by real matter, they could be gathered up and thrown outside one of the *Mole's* phantom ports. The *Mole* went on, still underground.

For a time, despite the terrific losses from those blasts, the police of Poughkeepsie were almost jubilant. Remembering Jack Hill's statement that violent explosions would come of the materialization of one solid body inside of another, it was thought that the explosions came from some such occurrence.

But they were undeceived. A quarter of a mile away, the earth heaved up. Further, it heaved up again. Durran took a terrible revenge for the attempt at resistance. When he left Poughkeepsie the shattered ruins behind him were a guarantee that no other city would ever attempt the use of radioactive bullets against the *Mole*. The casualty list in Poughkeepsie was six times as large as that in Albany. It shocked the world.

Next day, the *Mole* made no foray. And it was a strange fact that since the complete ruthlessness of the earth-ship's crew had been demonstrated, fewer hysterical reports of its presence were made. At first, perhaps, those who fancied they saw it made haste to tell the police in hopes of its capture. Now, they simply fled. But there is no verified report of any activity on Durran's part the day after the Poughkeepsie tragedy.

The day after, it struck Peekskill and Yonkers. It was plainly heading for New York and such an orgy of looting as no five men in the world had ever before engaged in. Another day of peace.

Then it invaded Brooklyn by way of Harlem, evidently passing under the East River in its progress. A night and day of wholesale looting, with the police standing helplessly by and as their only effort at defence preventing crowds from gathering where they could be slaughtered.

That was an ironic touch; that the police were so far from being able to counter Durran's criminal actions that the utmost they could do was prevent him from being annoyed while engaged in robbery.

New York was still untouched. And then, after a day and

a night of looting in Brooklyn, the motorman of a rush-hour Brooklyn subway express, slowing to a block signal in a tube under the river, saw the phantom, impossible apparition of the *Mole* lying across the tunnel. The only solid thing about it was the materializing tube Durran had invented and installed.

The motorman jammed on the air brakes and the cars behind him filled with noise as the standing passengers piled up in heaps. Then something came out of the round ring of solidity held upright by the phantom *Mole*. Something which looked white and flat, with a long ribbon attached to it. A light glowed in the materializing ring and shone down upon the dropped object. It was an envelope, a letter.

A guard, his teeth chattering, climbed out of the front door and picked it up. It was addressed to the mayor of Greater New York. Shivering, he climbed back into the subway train.

The *Mole* stirred. The motorman and those crowded to the front windows of the train could see through it, beyond it. A round thing dribbled out of the materializing tube and fell between the rails. Then there was a little flare of eerie light and the materializing tube vanished. The *Mole* swam serenely away through the solid walls of the tunnel. It was lost in the unexplored solidity beneath the bed of the river.

Then the round thing on the track flashed up. Tear gas filled all the tunnel. But the subway train had to go forward. It could not go back. Filled with blinded, hysterical passengers, it pulled into the first station on the Brooklyn side and its motorman made a ragged stop, judging only by the glare that a station was at hand.

The newspapers published extras, after that. The letter was a bland communication from Durran. He was holding New York to ransom. He would smash the subways and bridges, blast down the tall buildings by planting explosives at their bases, and wreck the water and power supply of the city if his terms were not met. And his terms were staggering. He gave the city forty-eight hours in which to agree to them. And as if to give point to his threat, within an hour an alarm came from the Brooklyn Navy Yard. The *Mole* was there. When it left, it had seized enough high explosives to blast down half of New York.

It was not especially comforting to receive a reassuring broadcast from the American Electric Co. saying that a full dozen earth-ships, each faster, more powerful, and more heavily armed than the original *Mole*, would be completed in ten days more. In that ten days, Durran would have ruined the city.

VII

Of course they sent for Jack Hill. In the governor's mansion at Albany he met with the mayor of New York City, the governor of the State, and an array of financial and industrial magnates who would have been impressive if they had not been so thoroughly panic-stricken.

Gail Kennedy was there, too. She'd insisted on coming back with Jack, and she and her father – now backing Jack strongly – provided moral support for him in the atmosphere of embittered hatred that filled the meeting.

'This is your fault!' said the mayor of New York furiously. 'The American Electric Co. financed the highly unwise experiments which have led to this grave menace to our commonwealth, but you built the piratical craft which now holds –'

Jack interrupted gently: 'You're talking nonsense. It may be good politics, but it's poor policy. Do you want to know what you ought to do?'

'That is what we have come here for. How far are we going to avoid meeting these impossible terms Durran imposes on our city?'

'Don't,' said Jack dryly. 'Pay him. You'll get it back.'

'How?'

'He can store only so much in the *Mole*,' replied Jack more dryly still. 'Even bank notes and bullion. As a matter of fact, bullion costs him money to carry around. My guess is that he's cached most of his loot, already. And my further guess is that the sweethearts of his four men have a pretty good idea where that cache is. When Durran and his men are killed – as they will be – those four women will spend some of it before they're caught, but not particularly much. Meanwhile, we gain time until the new earth-ships are finished.'

'But – millions and millions –' gasped a prominent banker.

'I have a suggestion to make,' said Jack gently, 'about the payment of that money. I will not make it in this mob' – even in such an emergency a rustle of indignation, a bristling, passed about the assembly – 'because I told an equally eminent group, some days ago, about a ship under construction to destroy the *Mole*. With really superlative fatheadedness, they told the world and consequently Durran. That ship was promptly blown up. So since you gentlemen can't be trusted to hold your tongues, I'll keep my own counsel until you've decided to meet Durran's terms. Then I'll communicate a suggestion to the person in charge of that payment. Not before!'

His idea was, of course, that bullion and even paper money could be so impregnated with radioactive material that when once taken on board the *Mole* it could not be moved through solidity and would expose the *Mole* to attack. A duplication, on a larger scale, of the incident of the radioactive bullets in Poughkeepsie.

'I might even,' Jack added sardonically, 'say that it's very possible that Durran knows where this meeting is taking place. If he does, and can make it here in time, we may be in a bad fix, anyhow, you and I and all of us.'

He swept his eyes about the gathering. Some of the faces looked frightened, some looked indignant, but none looked guilty. Jack felt reassured, which was a mistake. He did not realize that the sort of man who blabs a secret never feels guilty for having blabbed it. He feels only frightened, sometimes, for fear that it may be found out he has blabbed.

And Jack did not quite realize how many men have their price. Bribery is of no service in scientific research, and Jack's mind simply did not work in a fashion to understand it either as a method or a temptation.

'But do you realize that we're at the mercy of a pirate?' wailed a prominent Wall Street banker. 'Every cent –'

'With the warning you've had,' Jack broke in, 'I rather suspect you've shipped most of your valuables out of the city. At a guess, Durran's been in a couple of bank vaults and found them practically empty. Hence this holdup.'

'Of course!' snapped the mayor of New York. 'Most of the cash in New York has been shipped out. Most of the particularly valuable jewels, too. Even nine-tenths of the art treasures have gone!'

'Then there's nothing to be done –'

There was an indescribable noise outside – a strangled squawk, as if somebody saw something utterly terrifying. A lesser politician turned a ghastly white. Then something came through the door. The door was closed, but the Thing came through it. And suddenly whitish light flared, and a round ring appeared in mid-air.

The gathering of eminent figures in finance and politics became a howling, panic-stricken mob. A rush of fear-crazed men bowled Jack over. He struck out savagely and was on his feet again as something flashed from the floor. Jack fought ruthlessly, lifting Gail above a crazy tangle of struggling bodies. He thrust her feet first through a window to the terrace outside.

'Go on!' he snapped. 'Get in a car and speed!'

'Come with me! Quick!' she cried.

But he looked about him anxiously. He saw Gail's father plunge through the phantom body of the *Mole*; in its misty interior open the door of the conference room, and rush through to safety. Then swirling gas from the exploded bomb obliterated all sight.

Howls of pure panic arose about him. And Jack forced his way blindly through the window that had meant safety for Gail and tried to fumble his own way to some car with an unblinded driver. A horde of sightless, squealing men babbled and pushed. Crowded together, they had been bad enough. Opened out, now, they ran with flailing arms, hysterical with pure panic.

A fat man bumped against Jack, flinging him to one side. Somebody else struck crazily at him, and someone careened heavily into him, and he gave ground. Then, abruptly, there was something hard and unyielding against his knees, and he toppled over.

He fell perhaps eight feet, down from the terrace outside the windows of the governor's mansion. Branches lashed at him, and then he hit something incredibly hard and solid. He felt a terrific blow on his head.

A long time later, it seemed, Jack heard the purring of machinery. He heard Gail's voice, urgent and resolute. Somebody picked him up. The noise of machinery grew louder. It roared close beside him. He felt a swimming motion.

Then, as he stirred vaguely, something hit him again, and he passed into blank unconsciousness.

When Jack opened his eyes again the noise of machinery

still went on. There was again the sensation of swimming, of a gentle rocking from side to side. His head ached intolerably. Then his eyes cleared.

He was inside the *Mole*. His hands and feet were tied fast. Durran grinned at him. A rat-faced man with a convict's shaven poll was at the controls. Two others were in sight about the engine. But worst of all was the sight of Gail, very white, sitting in a crowded corner of the *Mole* and staring at vacancy.

VIII

Through the windows of the *Mole* the outside world could be seen. One glance, and Jack knew. A strange, harsh, reddish light outlined tall and unsubstantial columns reaching up to a roof of shadows. The columns rose from a cloudy, soft-seeming vapour underfoot. Over all and through all the reddish light showed.

The *Mole* swam on, and the columns swept slowly past, immobile despite their near transparency. There was no sound from without. The thudding rumble of the gasoline engine; the whine of the dynamo and the separate driving motors – that was all. There was not even a noise as of a water wash against the hull of the earth-ship. It swam on through an eerie, a phantom world – and it was almost impossible to believe.

Shadows even passed through the interior, through all its moving parts, through the human beings within it. They paid no heed. Those shadows were tree trunks, impalpable to the dematerialized state of the *Mole* as it was impalpable to the normal world.

Durran grinned and said: 'You're a very lucky young man.'

Jack opened his lips and closed them.

'I said,' repeated Durran amusedly, 'you're a very lucky young man. You're alive.'

'I hardly imagine,' returned Jack evenly, 'that I'll be alive very long.'

'It wasn't my intention to allow it,' conceded Durran. A mocking light danced in his eyes. 'Miss Kennedy persuaded me otherwise. You are very fortunate to have so charming a girl so – shall I say, loyal to you ?' He chuckled.

Jack was working on his bonds. Hopeless! They had been tied by someone who knew how.

'You want to know,' he said slowly, 'where the other earth-ships are being built to destroy you. That's why you brought me in the *Mole* instead of simply shooting me.'

'You guess,' said Durran, 'with remarkable accuracy.'

'Set her free,' said Jack grimly, 'and I'll tell you where they are. Otherwise you can go to hell! There's no power on earth that could make me tell while she's a prisoner.'

'I disagree,' said Durran. Again his eyes mocked. 'I think we could make you tell us anything. There are – er – methods. But I shan't try. I promised Miss Kennedy.'

Jack's eyes turned to Gail. She stood up and came over to him, bracing herself against the swaying movements of the *Mole*. She was silent for a moment. Then:

'I told him, Jack,' she said quietly. 'I – I wasn't blinded by the gas. You told me to run, but I – I waited to be sure you were safe. You – didn't come outside. I didn't see you, anyway. So I started to go back to find you. And the *Mole* swam out and materialized on the lawn. I hid. Then I saw two men get out and pick you up. I recognized you. And I ran –'

'She tried to fight us,' put in Durran blandly. 'And I recognized her, in turn. I had her showed inside the *Mole*, and of course we brought you in. We were very busy just about then, because there were police running to shoot at us. You were unconscious. I dematerialized the *Mole* and started to navigate away. And Miss Kennedy had picked up a hand grenade and swore she'd pull the pin and blow the lot of us to smithereens unless we released you at once.'

Again Jack's eyes turned upon Gail. 'Good girl!' he said grimly. 'I'm almost sorry that you didn't go through with it.'

'It was a stalemate,' said Durran as blandly as before. 'Because, as I pointed out, she'd do you no good by blowing us all up. Finally we compromised. I promised to release you, unharmed, but not her, if she'd put down the grenade, and if she told me where the other earth-ships are being built.'

'Jack, I – I had to! Don't you see? He promised to – only hold me for ransom.'

Durran nodded. 'That's all,' he said comfortably. 'You, Hill, will be allowed to leave the ship in ten minutes more. In fact, I'll insist on it.'

Jack searched his face. The mockery, the unholy amusement in his eyes, denied the promise of safety. There was no doubting that.

'Do you mean,' he asked harshly, 'you're going to re-materialize the ship and put me out on solid ground, or do you mean you're going to toss me out of the door into that?'

He nodded to the vapourous, unreal cloudiness which was the earth to those within the *Mole*.

'No!' said Gail quickly. 'He was laughing when he promised to let you out. I made him swear he didn't mean to put you out of the ship so you'd – drop down to the centre of the earth. He said you'd stay on top, all right.'

Durran laughed again.

'Well?' snapped Jack. 'What's the catch? And I tell you, Durran, no ransom you can get for her is as big as the one I can give you, of information you need! You turn her loose instead of me –'

'I'll let you decide,' said Durran blandly. 'You see, Hill, you gave advice on how to keep me from looting bank vaults by putting bars of iron about so I couldn't materialize any part of the *Mole* in a vault without including a bar and so blowing up the ship. The fools haven't taken your advice, but I thought they would.

'So I prepared for it.'

'How?'

'I made a field-of-force generator a man could carry into a vault, dodging those bars. He could dematerialize anything I wanted and bring it back without materializing the *Mole* inside at all and even without the *Mole's* entering it. It's a good trick. I can take things out of a drawer or the smallest safe, now. A neat answer to your suggestion. My men can walk about and pick up anything they want.'

Again Jack nodded grimly at the cloudlike earth. 'No man can walk about on that.'

'Oh, yes, a man can! You'll see! The same trick as the sustaining screws that hold this ship up. A thin coating of thorium. I made snowshoes, my dear fellow, on the same principle. Frames covered with cloth, which is painted with radioactive paint. We are going to get a pair of those snow-shoes for you. Earth-shoes would be a better name. With them upon your feet you can walk wherever you like. You can assuredly stay on top of the ground, even in your present state of dematerialization. Take my word for it – you can!'

Jack's eyes burned.

Gail stared, and then cried desperately: 'But – but you're cheating! He'd starve! And – and only as long as he kept moving. You're cheating! You'd be killing him as surely and – more horribly than if you just flung him out to drop.'

'But,' said Durran, and chuckled, 'I am holding to the strict letter of my bargain. I confess it seems to me an excellent joke. You have five minutes more, Hill, before you begin your interesting walk, unless you wish Miss Kennedy to have that freedom instead. How about it?'

Jack said grimly: 'Supposing you observe the proprieties and let a condemned man have a little indulgence. I want to talk to Gail. Clear out!'

Again Durran chuckled. 'And I'll do even that, instead of spending my time making just complaints about the manner in which you constructed the ship for me. My dear Hill, do you know that is is necessary to run the sustaining screws ten revolutions a minute faster than at the beginning? Why is that?'

'Repeated dematerializations,' snapped Jack. 'Clear out!'

He waited, his jaw set. Durran moved away, amused. It could not matter what Jack and Gail might say to each other. In five minutes more, Jack would be more utterly alone and more irrevocably doomed than any other man since time began. And Gail would remain the the *Mole*.

The cloudy shapes in the harsh red light without came to an end. The shadow of a house appeared, and beyond it a low and level mist more tenuous than that of earth. It would be the water of a lake.

The *Mole* swam smoothly up to the house. Then it seemed to glow in every particle with a strange white light, which gradually diminished and died. And as it diminished, the world without became more solid. When it ended, the shadow house became a bungalow. The cloudy earth was covered with green grass. The light was vastly brighter. And this normal, natural world looked infinitely desirable.

The rat-faced man got out of the ship and went casually into the house. Squeals of delight came out. Women appeared, five of them. And they were pretty women, in their fashion. But Jack looked from them to Gail and ground his teeth. The sight was too bitter.

The rat-faced man came back, carrying two cloth-covered frames which were nothing more or less than snowshoes of entirely familiar pattern, with painted canvas stoutly sewed to the rawhide webbing. He had told the women something. They laughed shrilly. He came into the *Mole* again. Again the flash of eerie, whitish light. The *Mole* swam on smoothly.

And then Durran threw a switch and reversed the tail screw. The moving procession of shadows in a world of harsh red light slowed down and stopped.

Durran opened the door of the *Mole*. 'And now I keep my promise,' he said blandly. 'You are free to go. In fact. if you don't go you'll be thrown out.'

Two men kept guns trained upon Jack as a third cut loose his hands. He put on the strange devices for walking in a world which was all vapour, all shadows, without substance or reality. To fight was not only hopeless, it would please Durran. And Jack had no hope, but he would not admit it. He pretended a confidence he did not feel, simply to make things easier for Gail.

'I'll see you later, Durran,' he said without intonation. 'I'm inclined to think you won't harm Gail, because I know what ransom you'll want. But I'll see you later!'

He stepped grimly out of the door. The stuff underfoot was soft and yielding and springy, but it seemed to give slowly from his weight. Actually, that was the thinly coated cloth sinking through the substance of the ground. If Jack stood still, he knew, he would sink down and down as into a quicksand. The earth was semisolid only to the devices upon his feet. To his body it was thin as air. If he stumbled, he would hang head down, swinging, and ultimately he would sink.

And then –

But he stood, balancing himself in a world all harsh red light and unreal shadows, with his weight resting upon the appearance of vapour. In all this universe only the *Mole* seemed real, because only the *Mole* was unreal where this world was actual.

Durran stood at a window and laughed at him. The door closed. The *Mole* swam away. Presently it was lost to sight amid the shadows of innumerable phantom trees. Jack was alone as no man had ever been alone before. He walked upon vapour, and about him were only ghosts.

IX

The silence was ear-cracking. Silence, in the normal world, is a compound of minute noises, each one of which contributes to a blended impression of quiet. Here there was an absolute absence of sound. It was startling. It was bewildering. There was constantly a shocked impression of one's own deafness.

Stranger still, of course, was the landscape. It was like a madman's dream. The sun was visible, to be sure, but as a ball of red so dark that it was almost purple. The unearthly light which filled this place was far down the scale, nearly in the infra-red. It was the darkest tint the human eye could see. In it, the trees were more than merely translucent.

Jack was seeing by rays which normally are blanketed out by the visible spectrum. The trees seemed so tenuous, so infinitely fragile that their immobility was not credible even when Jack saw it. And their branches went away to threads and their foliage stopped so little of the strange faint light that it seemed that overhead there was only the faintest of mist. Jack saw stars shining dully in an almost-black sky.

He had stopped, rather grimly, to orient himself. Now he essayed to move. And the ungainly things strapped to his feet were fast in the earth below him. That earth seemed vapour, to be sure. But there was radioactive paint upon these weird earth-shoes. That worked the miracle.

The flying alpha particles from that paint bombarded the dematerialized substance which alone in the world was real to Jack. The effect was that of temporary, partial materialization, so that the substance of the earth-shoes was partly 'real' in both states of matter.

Yet it was only partly 'real' so that it could still penetrate reality. But it did so slowly. Jack's earth-shoes had sunk a little, a very little, into the ground. But they would rise no more easily than they sank.

He felt a flash of panic, as a man might be expected to feel with a quicksand tugging at his legs. Then he forced himself to coolness. His feet had sunk perhaps six inches into the earth. He could not lift them. But he could slide them forward. He did. And the turned-up toes of the snowshoes helped, and a little later he strode forward through the impossible, a man walking upon a cloud, through shadows, beneath a sky and sun which did not seem of earth. He walked and moved, in fact, upon a world which had become itself a ghost in a universe that was phantom.

It was nightmarish, of course. It was worse than any nightmare. It was like insanity come true. And always, if he stood still, he would sink into the nightmare and strangle in the impalpable cloud which was the earth itself, and at last fall dizzily, twisting a little, down into the eternal fires which burned sullenly perhaps fifty, perhaps a hundred miles below him. But to think of that caused vertigo.

Jack headed east, holding a tight leash upon himself lest the panic which always clawed at him should seize his brain. There would be human beings to eastward. True, he would be a ghost to them, and they to him, but still – He forced himself to note all things with a careful attention. That way would come accustomedness.

· He suddenly realized that there were no smells in this strange universe. Again, like sounds, a man is normally unaware of tiny odours in the air he breathes. But their absence was strange. The air seemed strangely flat. It had the insipid flavour of boiled and hence tasteless water.

Then he saw something moving. His heart leaped for an instant. But this moving thing was itself a shadow. He watched it intently. It was a rabbit. He could look through its flesh and see the distinctly articulated, phantom bones within its mistlike body. Strangely, it seemed to see him, too. It leaped madly away. And Jack realized that, just as the rabbit seemed ghostlike to him, he would seem a ghost to it. Even more of a wraith and less visible, actually, because of the brighter light in the world of reality, whereby objects behind his no longer 'material' body would be so much more distinct.

He went on, without hope, but refusing to give way until he must. In this world of impalpable things there was no solid space on which he might rest. These was no food he could eat. There was no water he could lift to his lips or swallow. And he knew all this and trudged doggedly eastward, for no conceivable reason, for hour after hour. If he had any reason for his travail, it was that he could die without yielding to the panic Durran undoubtedly expected of him.

It was a ghastly journey. The earth-shoes upon his feet, clumsy and unaccustomed; the unearthly reddish light about him; the vaporous-seeming surface on which he walked; the knowledge of and the insistent nagging feeling of an abyss below him. He had no faintest idea of attaining to safety by this exertion. He knew the conditions under which hope might exist, and they were practically impossible. Without food or water or rest, with no means of communicating with any human being, with his loudest shout in the ear of a man but the faintest thread of a whisper – because he was a ghost –

A ghost!

Once he passed through a tiny country village. He saw ghosts about him, living in phantom houses, engaged in unreal tasks. He was unseen by humans, but dogs barked at him, frightened, terrified, the hackles at the top of their necks raised and bristling. Their barks were the faintest of whispers. He went on because their uproar made a phantom baby wake and wail soundlessly.

On – on.

He strode on for hours, desperately, watching without hope for something which might give hope. The dark-eyed, nearly purple, sun sank low. He had emerged from the phantom woods long since and now plodded across a vaporous open space which was featureless and unmeaning. The cloudiness rose above his earth-shoes, now. It was probably a growing crop of wheat or rye, unseeable save as mist. Ever and again he turned to look his last upon the sun. And very suddenly it vanished and all this unreal world was dark.

There were infinitely faint reddish lights in the sky over-head – stars. He stood upon a vapour that he could not see and that was not tangible to his hands. In all the world there was not one solid thing besides his body and the ungainly objects upon his feet. He was exhausted. He was weak with hunger and thirst and half mad with the knowledge of doom upon him and that impending drop down into the smouldering fires that burn eternally at the centre of the earth.

Two small red glows, like fireflies, swept through the blackness from a spot to the right of him. They moved almost before him and vanished abruptly. He plodded on. Two others. They were nearer. Again they vanished when before him. A curious tail of flickering flame seemed to follow them. He was almost too weary even to be curious. But somewhere in his brain a voice said:

'Motor cars. That tail of flame is the exhaust. It's hot enough to give off infra-red, and that's what you see by.'

He plodded on. Sooner or later he would stagger from the exhaustion that crept upon him. His muscles would refuse to obey him. He would stumble. He would fall –

Then he saw a row of dim red specks. They did not move. He regarded them dully. They would be the electric bulbs of a filling-station sign. He turned and moved drearily toward them. He would die, at least, near human beings he could not even signal to. He was very tired indeed. Presently the dim red specks stretched in the three sides of a rectangle above his head. That was the roof of the service cover. And the lights were probably very bright ones, because he made out very faintly indeed the phantom of the filling station itself. He walked through the walls of that phantom. A brighter reddish glow shone there – a round ring of light. No; two round rings of light. He regarded them apathetically. He was too tired to think clearly. He found himself reaching out his hand. He touched one of the rings of light. It burned him. It was, actually, the gasoline burner of a hot-dog boiler.

'Curious,' he said dully to himself. 'In theory, if it burned me, I must have affected the flame. And if there is a man near by – but there must be – I could signal to him if we both knew dots and dashes.'

Then he shrugged hopelessly. His finger hurt. It was severely scorched, but there was not enough light to see. He made a helpless gesture with his scorched hand – and the burned finger touched something solid.

For a moment he was dazed. Sheer shock made him dizzy. He touched the thing again. It was hot and scorched his burned finger. It was impalpable to the unburned ones.

Jack gasped. 'I feel – I feel a stove!'

Then he panted to himself, all alone in the unthinkable universe of his own discovery.

'Radioactivity knocks some of the atoms loose from their co-ordination. Fire, heat, ought to do the same thing. Especially if it caused chemical change – as it does when it scorches my skin. Heat demagnetizes steel, too. It ought to – it ought to materialize –'

He held his hand savagely to the flame. It was agony. It was torment. He scorched it all over, going sick from pain. And then he groped. He felt a wall. He fumbled, and fumbled –

The forty-eight hours given to the City of New York would expire at four p.m. At a little after three, Jack got rather stiffly out of a motorcycle side car at the isolated spot in New Jersey where the city's ransom was to be paid. The State trooper who'd brought him roared his machine away. Gail's father nodded to Jack, his face grey and drawn.

'I heard you were released,' he said jerkily, 'and that Gail was all right when you were turned loose.'

'She was all right,' said Jack composedly. 'But I wasn't turned loose in the way you mean. You're here to deliver the city's ransom?'

Kennedy nodded and licked his lips. 'I asked for the job,' he said desperately. 'I hope to see Gail and make terms with Durran for her release, too, you see.'

'He'll ask,' said Jack, 'for one of the new earth-ships. That's the price. I'm fairly sure.'

'He blew up four of them yesterday,' said Kennedy bitterly. 'They couldn't be moved as you wired they had to be. One was got away. He'll get the rest to-morrow, probably.'

Jack nodded. He got out a cigarette and lighted it. His fingers quivered like tuning forks.

'Listen!' he said suddenly.

He told Gail's father just how Gail had desperately bought his life by telling where the new earth-ships were being built. He told how Durran had cheated on the contract, amusedly, while holding to the strict letter of his agreement. He told of his horrible journey in that world which was not reality, and of the accidental discovery that the scorching of his own flesh would destroy the effect of the force field upon it, just as heat will destroy the magnetism of a bar of steel.

'I scorched my hand pretty thoroughly,' he finished, 'and felt around. I found the desk where the hot-dog man balanced up accounts. I found his pencil and wrote a message to him, telling who I was and how I came to be there. Then I attracted his attention by pounding his inkwell on the top of his desk.'

'Luckily, he wasn't just superstitious. He tried to find out what was happening. The radio broadcast had told about my being carried away in the *Mole*. The hot-dog man took a chance. He put his stove down on the floor, And I balanced myself on one of those earth-shoes and scorched the soles of my own leather shoes. I tried them. And the heat had rematerialized the bottom layer of the leather.

'I could stand on the floor of the hot-dog stand! At last I had some hope to cling to!

'Then I scorched the earth-shoes, too. The hot-dog man could see them, then. And they wouldn't sink through the floor at all. He believed me. I tore off bits of canvas that had been scorched. He could see them, too, and so could I. He put one over his ear as I'd told him to, in writing. One side was rematerialized by the heat. The other wasn't quite scorched and was real to me.

'I shouted at it. My voice vibrated my side of the cloth, and that made his side vibrate. In a little while he made me hear him, too, in the same way. We had to scream at each other, though with the hand I'd scorched I could touch him. It nearly scared him to death the first time I did it. Then he telephoned for me. And I lay down on the earth-shoes on the floor, and waited. The brought a force-field outfit and rematerialized me.

'I nearly keeled over when I saw the world actual about me again.'

Kennedy listened. He had to. But his thoughts were with Gail.

'But Gail –'

'Look at my hands.' said Jack jerkily. He held them out. They quivered. 'I found out something Durran doesn't know. It's a show-down. Either we get Gail back when Durran turns up, or – there's no hope for her at all.'

'What's the matter?'

'Durran's doomed,' said Jack unsteadily. 'He doesn't know it. I do. He told me he was having to run the sustaining screws ten revolutions a minute faster than at the beginning. And Gail's in the *Mole*. You see what that means?'

'No. What's happened?'

'The sustaining screws hold the *Mole* up,' replied Jack, puffing nervously, 'because they're coated with thorium. If it wasn't for that and their movement, the ship would drop like a stone. And the thorium plating is wearing off. Durran doesn't realize it, but the *Mole's* travelled a long way. When he's run it a certain time longer, so much of the plating will have worn off that no speed will enable the sustaining screws to hold the ship up. So we've got to get Gail out of the *Mole* to-day.' His eyes met the other's evenly.

Kennedy's face was grey and drawn. It went greyer yet. 'What are you going to do?'

'Ransom her,' replied Jack. 'If Durran sees me here, he won't go away leaving me alive. I hope he'll be curious enough to ask me how I escaped. Then I can talk to him. Did you see a plane sweep low across this place early this morning?'

Kennedy shook his head.

'It was supposed to dust the ground all about here,' said Jack jerkily. 'Like they dust crops by plane. That's part of the trick. I have the rest in my pocket. Where's the ransom for New York?'

Kennedy gestured toward half a dozen suitcases. 'Full of currency,' he said indifferently. 'State troopers all around us in a ring a couple of miles across. Durran's been looking over the place, we may be sure. He's probably watching us now.'

Jack nodded. He flung his cigarette away and lighted another.

'I've only about as long as it takes Durran to get here,' he said unsteadily, 'before I get bumped off. I'm hoping – I'm praying I get Gail clear. Only one chance, and that a thin one. But Durran goes, and I think I go with him.'

'But what are you going to do? demanded Kennedy desperately. 'What –' Then he stopped.

The *Mole*, a phantom, was rising out of the ground not a dozen yards away. It came fully into view, and the whitish, eerie light of the force field played upon it, diminishing. As it diminished, the *Mole* solidified. And as it solidified the screws found the earth in which they worked becoming more and more solid and they slowed and then finally stopped for the increased resistance.

The door opened. The ugly muzzle of a machine gun peered out.

'I've scouted pretty thoroughly,' said the voice of Durran harshly, 'and there's no trap here. I hope you didn't plan to have me bombed from the air, Kennedy. I've got your daughter with me.'

'N-no,' said Kennedy. He swallowed. 'I – I arranged to meet you so I could make terms for her ransom. Can I – speak to her?'

A pause.

Durran laughed. 'Why not? Go out, my dear, and talk to him. I can take you back any time I please –'

His voice broke off short. He'd recognized Jack.

'Hello, Durran,' said Jack coolly. 'You didn't like the last bargain I made with you. But it still stands as an offered ransom for Gail.'

Gail stepped out of the *Mole*, deathly white, and suddenly ran into her father's arms. She sobbed in sheer relief as she clung to him. 'Jack isn't dead!'

'Talk to you later, Gail,' said Jack evenly. 'I'm going to make a bargain for you to stay with your father.'

Durran found his voice again. 'The devil!' he said, shaken. 'I thought you were roasted long ago, Hill! I'll make sure you're dead before I leave this time!'

'Perhaps,' said Jack. 'I offered you information, while I was in the *Mole*, in exchange for Gail's safety. Kill me and you don't get it. It's about – this.'

He took a flat package, about the size of a tobacco tin, out of his pocket. The ugly muzzle of the machine gun swung and covered him accurately.

You're covered,' said Durran. 'What's the trick?'

'You can't dematerialize within a certain distance of one of these contrivances,' said Jack. 'They're being turned out in quantity. The result is that if you materialize anywhere these things have been planted, you can't get away and are subject to attack. I'll trade full information, and come with you to give it, for Gail's release. Maybe you can beat them. I doubt it. But you can work out a detector for them, if you know how they work.'

'That's impossible!' snapped Durran.

'So is the *Mole*.' submitted Jack. 'You can't dematerialize your ship right now. Isn't the secret of that trick worth Gail's release?'

A pause.

Durran's voice sounded suspicious. 'If it's true. That might be a bomb, though. You stay where you are. I'm going to test it out. This machine gun stays trained on you. I turn on the force field. If you lie, I can materialize again fast enough to kill you.'

'But you can't dematerialize,' said Jack. He smiled faintly. 'You're inside the range of this thing.'

Only a grunt came from inside the *Mole*. Something

rumbled within. The sustaining screws stirred. Instantly the ship flashed into the state of co-ordinated atoms, they would whir swiftly, looking like the most tenuous of froth but sustaining the whole weight of the earth-ship.

'If you dare move,' said Durran harshly, 'I'll kill all three of you!'

Then the *Mole* flared with eerie, whitish light. It became a phantom.

And it dropped with a headlong swiftness at one and the same instant. One instant there was the *Mole*, all solid, riveted, bullet-scarred plates of steel. Next instant there was a glowing outline which fell as it glowed. Then there was nothing. No phantom. No outline. Nothing.

Jack smiled very, very faintly. 'I think,' he said softly, 'that's that!'

Gail stared at him. 'Jack! Where's the *Mole* ?'

Jack said rather grimly: 'The thorium plating on the sustaining screws has been wearing thin. So this morning I had a plane fly low over this place Durran had appointed. It dusted all the top of the ground with crystals of phosphoric acid. There's been rain lately, and the ground is moist. The acid made a strong solution in all the top soil. And the *Mole* came swimming through that soil. As long as it was dematerialized, of course, the acid did nothing. But when the *Mole* materialized, the phosphoric acid dissolved off the remaining thin plating of thorium from the screws. And I persuaded Durran to dematerialize – and there was nothing to hold the ship up. It fell through earth and stone. It's still falling. We'll never see Durran again.'

Gail said, absurdly: 'Jack! The *Mole* you built! It's gone!'

'Yes,' said Jack. 'And I expected to be in it. I was sure Durran would make me come in, but he was afraid that "contrivance" was a bomb. It was, and I've another in my pocket. With you outside of the *Mole* and me inside with two bombs – I told your father Durran would go. He – had to be finished.'

But he looked rather sick. The *Mole* would still be falling – toward those smouldering internal fires to which Durran had doomed him once.

Then, quite suddenly, the ground trembled. A distant, muted, racking sound came from far, far underground. It ceased.

'That – that ends it,' said Jack. 'Durran knew what he was falling to. He was clever. He probably even figured out what I did. So he blew up the ship rather than wait. I'm rather glad of that.'

Silence! Little rustling noises of leaves and grass in the wind.

Then Kennedy said fiercely: 'That's done with, then! Durran's finished! And we'll get back to work! You, Jack, you'll be needed to explain that earth-plane idea. We'll have under-ocean passenger service to Europe within a year. We'll have fleets of earth-planes moving through solidity, safer than aeroplanes or ships could be. And we'll be mining ten and twenty miles deep with those mine cages you talked about –'

But Gail let go of her father's hands. She walked over to Jack and into his arms.

'My father thinks you've made good, Jack,' she told him. 'Now, you tell him there's something very important to be attended to before you do any more work on those nasty earth-ships!'

Jack pressed her close.

'Yes; there is. Do you mind attending a wedding this afternoon, sir?' he asked Kennedy.

'Not at all,' replied Kennedy with a grimace. 'You two stay here a moment while I get those State police. Watch these bags, if you can. The ransom for New York is in them. It's got to be taken back.'

The Moon Era
JACK WILLIAMSON

I

We were seated at dinner in the long dining room of my uncle's Long Island mansion. There was glistening silver plate, and the meal had been served with a formality to which I was unaccustomed. I was ill at ease, though my uncle and I sat alone at the table. The business of eating, without committing an egregious blunder before the several servants, took all my attention.

It was the first time I had ever seen my uncle, Enfield Conway. A tall man, stiffly erect, dressed severely in black. His face, though lean, was not emaciated as is usual at his age of seventy years. His hair, though almost perfectly white, was abundant, parted on the side. His eyes were blue, and strong; he wore no glasses.

A uniformed chauffeur had met me at the station, in the afternoon. The butler had sent an entirely unnecessary valet to my luxurious room. I had not met my uncle until he came down to the dining room.

'I suppose, Stephen, you are wondering why I sent for you,' he said in his precise manner, when the servants had carried away the last course, leaving cigars, and a bottle of mineral water for him.

I nodded. I had been instructor of history in a small high school in Texas, where his telegram had reached me. There had been no explanation; merely a summons to Lond Island.

'You are aware that some of my patents have been quite profitable.'

Again I nodded. 'The evidence surrounds me.'

'Stephen, my fortune amounts to upwards of three-and-a-half million. How should you like to be my heir?'

'Why, sir – I should not refuse. I'd like very much to be.'

'You can, if you wish, earn that fortune. And fifty thousand a year while I live.'

I pushed back the chair and rose to my feet in excitement. Such riches were beyond my dreams! I felt myself trembling.

'Anything –' I stammered. 'I'll do anything you say, to earn that! It means –'

'Wait,' he said, looking at me calmly. 'You don't know yet what I require. Don't commit yourself too soon.'

'What is it?' I asked, in a quivering voice.

'Stephen, I have been working in my private laboratory here for eleven years. I have been building a machine. The best of my brains have gone into that machine. Hundreds of thousands of dollars. The efforts of able engineers and skilled mechanics.

'Now the machine is finished. It is to be tested. The engineers who worked with me refused to try the machine. They insist that it is very dangerous.

'And I am too old to make the trial. It will take a young man, with strength, endurance, and courage.

'You are young, Stephen. You look vigorous enough. I suppose your health is good? A sound heart? That's the main thing.'

'I think so,' I told him. 'I've been coaching the Midland football team. And it isn't many years since I was playing college football, myself.'

'And you have no dependants?'

'None – But what is this machine?'

'I will show you. Come.'

He rose, agilely enough for one of his seventy years, and led the way from the long room. Through several magnificent rooms of the big house. Out into the wide, landscaped grounds, beautiful and still in the moonlight.

I followed silently. My brain was confusion. A whirl of mad thought. All this wealth whose evidence surrounded me might be my own! I cared nothing for luxury, for money itself. But the fortune would mean freedom from the thankless toil of pedagogy. Books. Travel. Why I could see with my own eyes the scenes of history's dramatic moments! Finance research expeditions of my own! Delve with my own hands for the secrets of Egypt's sands, uncover the age-old enigmas of ruined mounds that once were proud cities of the East!

We approached a rough building – resembling an aeroplane hangar – of galvanised iron, which glistened like silver in the rays of the full moon.

Without speaking, Uncle Enfield produced a key from his pocket, unlocked the heavy padlock on the door. He entered the building, switching on electric lights inside it.

'Come in,' he said. 'Here it is. I'll explain it as well as I can.'

I walked through the narrow doorway and uttered an involuntary exclamation of surprise at sight of the huge machine that rested upon the clean concrete floor.

Two huge discs of copper, with a cylinder of bright, chromium-plated metal between them. Its shape vaguely suggested that of an ordinary spool of adhesive plaster, from which a little has been used – the polished cylinder, which was of smaller diameter than the discs, took the place of the roll of plaster.

The lower of the massive discs rested on the concrete floor. Its diameter was about twenty feet. The cylinder above it was about sixteen feet in diameter, and eight feet high. The copper disc above was the same size as the lower one.

Small round windows stared from the riveted metal plates forming the cylinder. The whole was like a building, it burst on me. A circular room with bright metal walls. Copper floor and copper roof projecting beyond those walls.

My uncle walked to the other side of this astounding mechanism. He turned a projecting knob. An oval door, four feet high, swung inward in the curving wall. Four inches thick. Of plated steel. Fitting very tightly against cushions of rubber.

My uncle climbed through the door, into the dark interior. I followed with a growing sense of wonder and excitement. I groped toward him through the darkness. Then I heard the click of a switch, and lights flashed on within the round chamber.

I gazed about me in astonishment.

Walls, floor, and ceiling were covered with soft, white fibre. The little room was crowded with apparatus. Clamped against one white wall was a row of the tall steel flasks in which commercial oxygen is compressed. Across the room was a bank of storage batteries. The walls were hung with numerous instruments, all clamped neatly in place. Sextants. Compasses. Pressure gauges. Numerous dials whose functions were not apparent. Cooking utensils. An automatic pistol. Cameras. Telescopes. Binoculars.

In the centre of the room stood a table or cabinet, with switches, dials, and levers upon its top. A heavy cable, apparently of aluminium, ran from it to the ceiling.

I was gazing about in bewilderment. 'I don't understand all this –' I began.

Naturally,' said my uncle. 'It is quite a novel invention. Even the engineers who built it did not understand it. I confess that the theory of it is yet beyond me. But what happens is quite simple.

'Eleven years ago, Stephen, I discovered a new phenomenon. I had happened to charge two parallel copper plates, whose distances apart had a certain very definite relation to their combined masses, with a high tension current at a certain frequency.

'The plates, Stephen, were in some way – how, I do not pretent to understand – cut out of the earth's gravitational field. Insulated from gravity. The effect extended to any object placed between them. By a slight variation of the current's strength, I was able to increase the repulsion, until the plates pulled upward with a force approximately equal to their own weight.

'My efforts to discover the reason for this phenomenon – it is referred to in my notes as the Conway Effect – have not been successful. But I have built this machine to make a practical application of it. Now that it is finished, the four engineers who helped design it have deserted. They refused to assist with any trials.'

'Why?' I asked.

'Muller, who had the construction in charge, somehow came to the conclusion that the suspension or reversal of gravity was due to motion in a fourth dimension. He claimed that he had experimental proof of his theory, by building models of the device, setting the dials, and causing them to vanish. I would have none of it. But the other men seemed to accept his ideas. At any rate, they refused with him to have any part in the tests. They thought they would vanish, like Muller says his models did, and not come back.'

'The thing is supposed to rise above the ground?' I asked.

'Quite so.' My uncle smiled. 'When the force of gravitation is merely suspended, it should fly off the earth at a tangent, due to the diurnal rotation. This initial velocity, which in these latitudes, amounts to considerably less than one thousand miles per hour, can be built up at will, by reversing gravitation, and falling away from the earth.'

'*Falling away from the earth!*' I was staggered. 'And where is one to fall.'

'This machine was designed for a trip to the moon. At the beginning of the voyage, gravitation will be merely cut out, allowing the machine to fly off on a tangent, toward the point of intersection with the moon's orbit. Safely beyond the atmosphere, repulsion can be used to build up the acceleration. Within the gravitational sphere of the moon, positive gravitation can be utilized further to increase the speed. And reversed gravitation to retard the velocity, to make possible a safe landing. The return will be made in the same manner.'

I was staring at him blankly. A trip to the moon seemed insane, beyond reason. Especially for a professor of history, with only a modicum of scientific knowledge. And it must be dangerous, if those engineers –. But three million – what dangers would I not face for such a fortune?

'Everything has been done,' he went on, 'to ensure the comfort and safety of the passenger. The walls are insulated with a fibre composition especially worked out to afford protection from the cold of space, and from the unshielded radiation of the sun. The steel armour is strong enough not only to hold the necessary air pressure, but to stop any ordinary meteoric particles.

'You notice the oxygen cylinders, for maintaining that essential element in the air. There is automatic apparatus for purifying it. It is pumped through caustic soda to absorb the carbon dioxide, and through refrigerator tubes to condense the excess moisture.

'The batteries, besides energizing the plates, are amply powerful to supply light and heat for cooking.

'That, I believe, fairly outlines the machine and the projected voyage. Now it is up to you. Take time to consider it fully. Ask me any questions you wish.'

He sat down deliverately in the large, cushioned chair, beside the central table, which was evidently intended for the operator. He stared at me alertly, with calm blue eyes.

I was extremely agitated. My knees had a weak feeling, so that I desired to sit down also; though I was so nervous that

I kept striding back and forth across the resilient white fibre of the floor.

Three millions! It would mean so much! Books, magazines, maps – I should have to economize no longer. Years – all my life, if I wished – abroad. The tombs of Egypt. The sand-covered cities of the Gobi. My theory that mankind originated in South Africa. All those puzzles that I had longed to be able to study. Stonehenge! Angkor! Easter Island!

But the adventure seemed madness. A voyage to the moon! In a craft condemned by the very engineers that had built it. To be hurled away from the earth at speeds no man had attained before. To face unknown perils of space. Dangers beyond guessing. Hurtling meteors. The all-penetrating cosmic ray. The burning heat of the sun. The absolute zero. What, beyond speculation and theory, did men know of space? I was no astronomer; how was I to cope with the emergencies that might rise?

'How long will it take?' I demanded suddenly.

My uncle smiled a little. 'Glad you are taking it seriously,' he said. 'The duration of the voyage depends on the speed you make, of course. A week each way is a conservative estimate. And perhaps two or three days on the moon. To take notes. Photograph it. Move around a little, if possible; land in several different places. There is oxygen and concentrated food to last six months. But a fortnight should see you nearly back. I'll go over the charts and calculations with you.'

'Can I leave the machine on the moon?'

'No, No atmosphere. And it would be too hot in the day, too cold at night. Of course an insulated suit and oxygen mask might be devised. Something like diving armour. But I haven't worked at that. You will be expected just to take a few pictures, be prepared to describe what you have seen.'

I continued to pace the floor, pausing sometimes to examine some piece of apparatus. How would it feel, I wondered, to be shut up in here? Drifting in space. Far from the world of my birth. Alone. In silence. Entombed. Would it not drive me mad?

My uncle rose suddenly from the chair.

'Sleep on it, Stephen,' he advised. 'See how you feel in the morning. Or take longer if you wish.'

He switched off the light in the machine. Led the way out into the shed. And from it into the brilliant moonlight that flooded the wide, magnificent grounds about the great house that would be one of the prizes of this mad adventure.

As he was locking the shed, I gazed up at the moon.

Broad, bright disc. Silvery, mottled. Extinguishing the stars with argent splendour. And all at once it came over me – the desire to penetrate the enigmatic mystery of this companion world, that men have watched since the race began.

What an adventure? To be the first human to tread this silver plant. To be the first to solve its age-old riddles. Why think of Angkor, or Stonehenge, of Luxor and Karnak, when I might win the secrets of the moon?

Even if death came, what did it matter against the call of this adventure? Many men would trade their lives eagerly for such a chance.

Suddenly I was strong. All weakness had left me. All fear and doubt. A few moments before I had been tired, wishing to sit down. Now vast energy filled me. I was conscious of an extraordinary elation. Swiftly I turned to my uncle.

'Let's go back,' I said. 'Show me as much about it as you can tonight. I am going.'

He gripped my hand tightly, without a word, before he turned back to the lock.

II

TOWARD THE MOON

It was in the second week, after that sudden decision came to me, that I started. At the end my uncle became a little alarmed, and tried to persuade me to stay longer, to make more elaborate preparations. I believe that he was secretly becoming fond of me, despite his brisk precise manner. I think he took the opinion of his engineers seriously enough to consider my return very uncertain.

But I could see no reason for longer delay. The operation of the machine was simple; he had explained it quite fully.

There was a switch to close, to send current from the batteries through the coils that raised it to the potential necessary to energize the copper discs. And a large rheostat that controlled the force, from a slight decrease in gravity, to a complete reversal.

The auxiliary apparatus, for control of temperature and atmosphere, was largely automatic. And not beyond my limited mechanical comprehension. I was certain that I should be able to make any necessary repairs or adjustments.

Now I was filled with the greatest haste to undertake the adventure. No doubt or hesitation had troubled me since the moment of the decision. I felt only a longing to be sweeping away from the earth. To view scenes that the ages had kept hidden from human eyes; to tread the world that has always been the symbol of the unattainable.

My uncle recalled one of the engineers, a sallow young fellow named Gorton. On the second morning, to supplement my uncle's instruction, he went over the machine again, showing me the function of every part. Before he left, he warned me.

'If you are idiot enough to get in that darned contraption, and turn on the power,' he told me, 'you'll never come back. Muller said so. And he proved it. So long as the batteries and coil are outside the field of force between the plates, the plates act according to schedule, and rise up in the air.

'But Muller made self-contained models. With the battery and all inside. And they didn't rise up. They went out! Vanished. Just like that!' He snapped his fingers.

'Muller said the things moved along another dimension, right out of our world. And he ought to know. String of degrees a mile long. Into another dimension. No telling what sort of hell you'll blunder into.'

I thanked the man. But his warnings only increased my eagerness. I was about to tear aside the veil of the unknown. What if I did blunder into new worlds? Might they not yield rewards of knowledge richer than those of the barren moon? I might be a new Columbus, a greater Balboa.

I slept a few hours in the afternoon, after Gorton had gone. I felt no conscious need of slumber, but my uncle insisted upon it. And to my surprise, I fell soundly asleep, almost as soon as I lay down.

At sunset, we went down again to the shed in which the machine was housed. My uncle started a motor, which opened the roof like a pair of enormous doors, by means of pulleys and cables. The red light of the vening sky streamed down upon the machine.

We made a final inspection of all the apparatus. My uncle explained again the charts and instruments that I was to use in navigating space. Finally he questioned me for an hour, making me explain the various parts of the machine, correcting any error.

I was not to start until nearly midnight.

We returned to the house, where an elaborate dinner was waiting. I ate almost absently, hardly noticing the servants of whom I had been so conscious upon my arrival. My uncle was full of conversation, Talking of his own life, and asking me many questions about my own, and about my father, whom he had seen last when they were boys. My mind was upon the adventure before me; I could answer him only disjointedly. But I was aware that he had taken a real liking for me; I was not surprised at his request that I postpone the departure.

At last we went back down to the machine. The white moon was high; its soft radiance bathed the gleaming machine, through the opened roof. I stared up at its bright disc. Was it possible that in a short week I should be there, looking back upon the earth? It seemed madness! But the madness of glorious adventure!

Without hesitation, I clambered through the oval door. A last time my uncle wrung my hand. He had tears in his eyes. And his voice was a little husky.

'I want you to come back, Stephen.'

I swung the door into its cushioned seat, upon massive hinges, tightened the screws that were to hold it. A final glance about the white-walled interior of the machine. All was in order. The chronometer by the wall, ticking steadily, told me that the moment had come.

My uncle's anxious face was pressed against one of the ports. I smiled at him. Waved. His hand moved across the port. He left the shed.

I dropped into the big chair beside the table, reached for the switch. With my fingers upon the button, I hesitated the merest second. Was there anything else? Anything neglected? Anything I had yet to do on earth? Was I ready to die, if so I must?

The deep, vibrant hum of the coils, beneath the table, answered the pressure of my finger. I took the handle of the rheostat, swung it to the zero mark, where gravitation was to be cut off completely.

My sensation was exactly as if the chair, the floor, had fallen from under me. The same sensation that one feels when an elevator drops very abruptly. Almost I floated out of the chair. I had to grasp at the arm of it to stay within it.

For a few moments I experienced nauseating vertigo. The white crowded room seemed to spin about me. To drop away endlessly beneath me. Sick, helpless, miserable, I clung weakly to the great chair. Falling . . . falling . . . falling. Would I never strike bottom?

Then I realized, with relief, that the sensation was due merely to the absence of gravity's familiar pull. The machine had worked! My last, lingering doubt was killed. Strange elation filled me.

I was flying away from the earth. Flying.

The thought seemed to work a miracle of change in my feelings. The dreadful, dizzy nausea gave way to a feeling of exhilaration. Of lightness. I was filled with a sense of power and well-being, such as I had never before experienced.

I left the great chair, floated rather than walked to one of the windows.

Already I was high in the air. So high that the moonlit earth was a dim and misty plain before me. I could see many lights; the westward sky was aglow, above New York. But already I was unable to pick out the lights at my uncle's mansion.

The machine had risen through the opened roof of the shed. It was driving out into space, as it had been planned to do! The adventure was succeeding.

As I watched, the earth sank visibly. Became a great concave bowl of misty silver. Expanded slowly, as the minutes went by. And became suddenly convex. A huge dark sphere, washed with pale grey light.

Presently, after an hour, when the dials showed that I was beyond the faintest trace of atmosphere, I returned to the table and increased the power, moving the rheostat to the last contact. I looked at charts and chronometer. According to my uncle's calculations, four hours as this acceleration were required, before the controls were set again.

I returned to the window and stared in amazement at the earth, that I had left vast and silver grey and motionless.

It was spinning madly, backwards!

The continents seemed to race beneath me – I was now

high enough to see a vast section of the globe. Asia. North America. Europe. Asia again. In seconds.

It was madness! The earth spinning in a few moments, instead of the usual twenty-four hours. And turning backward! But I could not doubt my eyes. Even as I watched, the planet seemed to spin faster. Even faster! The continental outlines merged into dim indistinctness.

I looked away from the mad earth, in bewilderment. The firmament was very black. And the very stars were creeping about it, with visible motions!

Then the sun came into view, plunging across the sky like a flaming comet. It swung supernally across my field of vision, vanished. Appeared again. And again. Its motion became ever swifter.

What was the meaning of such an apparent revolution of the sun about the sky? It meant, I knew, that earth and moon had swung about the star. That a year had passed! But were years going by as fast as my chronometer ticked off the seconds?

Another strainge thing. I could recognize the constellations of the Zodiac, through which the sun was plunging. And it was going backward! As the earth was spinning backward!

I moved to another window, searched for the moon, my goal. It hung still among spinning stars. But in its light there was a flicker, far more rapid than the flashing of the sun across the wild heavens. I wondered, then knew that I saw the waxing and waving of the moon. Months, passing so swiftly that soon the flicker became a grey blur.

The flashing past of the sun became more frequent. Until it was a strange belt of flame about the strange heavens, in which the stars crept and moved like living things.

A universe gone mad! Suns and planets spinning helpless in the might of a cosmic storm! The machine from which I watched the only sane thing in a runaway cosmos!

Then reason came to my rescue.

Earth, moon, sun, and stars could not all be mad. The trouble was with *myself!* My perceptions had changed. The machine –

Slowly it came to me, until I knew I had grasped the truth.

Time, true time, is measured by the movements of the heavenly bodies. Our day is the time of earth's rotation on its axis. Our year the period of its revolution about the sun.

Those intervals had become crowded so thick in my perception that they were indistinguishable. Then countless years were spinning past, while I hung still in space!

Incredible! But the conclusion was inevitable.

And the apparent motion of earth and sun had been backward.

That meant – and the thought was staggering – that the ages were reeling backward. That I was plunging at an incalculable rate into the past.

Vaguely I recalled magazine articles that I had read, upon the nature of space and time. A lecture. The subject had fascinated me, though I had only a layman's knowledge of it.

The lecturer had defined our universe in terms of space-time. A four-dimensional 'continuum'. Time was a fourth dimension, he had said. An extension as real as the three of what we call space, and not completely distinguishable from them. A direction in which motion would carry one into the past, or into the future.

All memory, he had said, is a groping back along this dimension, at right angles to each of the three of space. Dreams, vivid memories, he insisted, carry one's consciousness in reality back along this dimension, until the body, swept relentlessly along the stream of time, drags it forward again.

Then I recalled what my uncle had told me of the refusal of his engineers to try the machine. Recalled Gorton's warning. Muller, they both had told me, had declared that the machine would move along a fourth dimension, out of our world. He had made models of the machine, and they had vanished when the power was turned on.

Now I knew that Muller was right. His models had vanished because they had been carried into the past. Had not continued to exist in the present time.

And now I was moving along that fourth dimension. The dimension of time. And very swiftly, for the years went past too fast for counting.

The reversal of gravitation, it came to me, must be some effect of this change of direction in time. But I am not a scientist, I can explain the "Conway Effect" no better than my uncle, for all the wonders that it has brought into my life.

At first it was horribly strange and terrifying.

After I had thought out my explanation of the mad antics

131

of the earth and sun and moon, and of the hurrying stars, I was, however, no longer frightened. I gazed out through my small round ports at the melting firmament with some degree of equanimity.

I continued to watch the charts my uncle had prepared, and to make adjustments of the rheostat when they were indicated by the chronometer.

And presently, feeling hungry, I toasted biscuits on the electric stove, cut off a generous slice of cheese that I found in the supplies, opened a vacuum bottle of steaming chocolate, and made a hearty and very satisfactory meal.

When I had finished, the aspect of the space about me was unchanged. Crawling stars, already forming themselves into constellations the most of which were unfamiliar. The sun a broad belt of burning gold, counting off the years too swiftly for the eye to follow. A living flame that girdled the firmament. The earth was a huge grey sphere, spinning so swiftly behind me that no detail was visible.

And even the moon, hanging in space ahead, was turning slowly. No longer was the same familiar face toward me, and toward the earth. Already I had reached a point in past time at which the moon was turning on its axis more rapidly than it revolved about the earth. The tidal drag had not yet completely stopped the moon's apparent rotation.

And if already the moon was turning, what would it be when I reached it? Hurtling into the past as I was, would I see oceans cover its dry sea floors? Would I see an atmosphere soften the harsh outlines of its rugged mountains? Would I see life, vegetation, spread over its plains? Was I to witness the rejuvenation of an aged world?

It seemed fantastic. But it was taking place. The speed of rotation slowly increased as I watched.

The hours slipped past.

I became heavy with sleep. The two days before the departure had not been easy. I had worked day and night to familiarize myself with the machine's operation. The nervous strain had been exhausting. The amazing incidents of the voyage had kept me tense, sapped my strength.

The chart told me that no change was to be made in the controls for many hours. I inspected the gauges which showed the condition of the atmosphere in the chamber. Oxygen content, humidity, temperature, were correct. The air smelled sweet and clean. I completed the rounds, found everything in order.

I adjusted the big chair to a reclining position, and threw myself upon it. For hours I slept, waking at intervals to make a tour of inspection.

Sometimes, in the following days, I wondered if I should be able to go back. Muller's models had carried no operator, of course to start them on the flight back through time to the starting point. Would I be able to reverse the time-flight? If I followed the directions on the operating chart, on the flight back, would I be flung forward through the ages, back to my own era?

I wondered. But the speculation brought forth no conclusion. A strange, unique experience was mine. Glorious adventure. Death was not too high a price to pay.

It did not even occur to me to attempt to turn back earthward, when I found that I was slipping through time. And I did not have sufficient control of the machine to have done so, had I wished. Dependent upon the chart for navigating instructions, I could not have plotted a return path from the midway point. And I knew no way to stop my flight, except by using the repulsion of the moon's reversed gravitation.

My flight lasted six days, by the chronometer.

Long before the end, the moon was spinning very swiftly. And the edges of its outline had become hazy, so that I knew it had an atmosphere.

I followed the charted directions, until I was in the upper layers of that atmosphere. The moon's surface was sliding very rapidly beneath me, and the atmosphere with it, due to the swift rotation of the satellite. Consequently, fierce winds screamed about the machine.

I hung in the atmosphere, merely using enough power to balance the moon's comparatively feeble gravitational pull, until the pressure of that rushing wind swept me with it. The mistily indistinct surface slowed, became motionless beneath me.

With power decreased still further, I settled slowly, watching alertly through the ports.

A towering, crimson mountain loomed above the mist below. I dropped toward it, increasing the power a little. At last I hovered motionless above a narrow, irregular plateau, near the peak, that seemed covered with soft scarlet moss.

Slowly I cut down the power. With hardly a shock, the machine settled in the moss.

I was on the moon! The first of my race to set foot upon an alien planet! What adventures might await me?

III

WHEN THE MOON WAS YOUNG

With the power cut off entirely, I ran to the ports. There had been no time to scan my surroundings during the uncertainties of the landing. Now I peered out eagerly.

The moonscape was as strange a sight as man had ever seen.

The machine had come down in thick green moss, that looked soft as a Persian rug. A foot deep it was. Dark green fibres closely intertwined. In an unbroken carpet it covered the sloping plateau upon which I had landed, and extended almost to the top of the rugged peak to northward.

To the south and west lay a great valley, almost level, miles across. Beyond it rose a dim range of green hills, rugged summits bare and black. A broad river, glinting white in the distance, flowed down the valley, from northwest, into the south. Then there must be an ocean in that direction.

Strange jungle covered that valley, below the green moss of the mountains. Masses of green. Walls of yellow lining the wide smooth river. Dense forests of gigantic plants, weirdly and grotesquely strange. They grew more luxuriant, taller, than similar plants could upon the earth, because a much feebler gravitation opposed their growth.

Equally strange was the sky.

Darker than on earth, perhaps because the atmosphere was thinner. A deep, pure, living blue. A blue that was almost violet. No cloud marred its liquid azure splendour.

The sun hung in the glorious eastward sky. Larger than I had known it. Whiter. A supernal sphere of pure white flame.

Low in the west was an amazing disc. A huge ball of white, a globe of milky light. Many times the diameter of the sun. I wondered at it. And realized that it was – the earth! The earth young as Venus had been in my time. And like Venus, shrouded in white clouds never broken. Were the rocks still glowing beneath those clouds, I wondered? Or had the life begun – the life of my farthest progenitors?

Would I ever see my native land again, upon that resplendent, cloud-hidden planet? Would the machine carry me back into the future, when I attempted return? Or would it hurl me farther into the past, to plunge flaming into the new-born and incandescent world?

That question I put resolutely from my mind. A new world was before me. A globe strange and unexplored. Why worry about return to the old?

My eyes went back to the broad valley below me, along the banks of the broad river, beneath the majestic range of green mountains, Clumps of gold, resembling distant groves of yellow trees. Patches of green that looked like meadows of grass. Queer, puzzling uprights of black.

I saw things moving. Little bright objects, that rose and fell slightly as they flew. Birds? Gigantic insects? Or creatures stranger than either?

Then I saw the balloons. Captive balloons, floating above the jungles of the valley. At first I saw only two, hanging side by side, swaying a little. Then three more, beyond. Then I distinguished dozens, scores of them, scattered all over the valley.

I strained my eyes at them. Were there intelligent beings here, who had invented the balloons? But what would be the object of hanging them above the jungles, by the hundred.

I remembered the powerful prism binoculars hanging on the wall beside me. I seized them, focused them hurriedly. The weird jungle leaped toward me in the lenses.

The things were doubtless balloons. Huge spheres of purple, very bright in the sunlight. Anchored with long red cables. Some of them, I estimated, were thirty feet in diameter. Some, much smaller. I could make out no baskets. But there seemed to be small dark masses upon their lower sides, to which the red ropes were attached.

I left them and surveyed the jungle again.

A mass of the yellow vegetation filled the lenses. A dense tangle of slender yellow stems, armed with terrible rows of long, bayonet-like thorns. A thick tangle of sharp yellow thorns, it seemed, with no more stalk than was necessary to support them against the moon's feeble pull. A wall of cruel spikes, impenetrable.

I found a patch of green. A mass of soft, feathery foliage. A sort of creeper, it seemed, covering rocks, and other vegetation – though it did not mingle with the yellow scrub. Enormous, brilliantly white, bell-shaped blooms were open upon it here and there.

A flying thing darted across my vision. It looked like a gigantic moth, frail wings dusted with silver.

Then I made out a little cluster of curious plants. Black, smooth, upright stalks, devoid of leaf or branch. The tallest looked a foot in diameter, a score in height. It was crowned with a gorgeous red bloom. I noticed that no other vegetation grew near any of them. About each was a little cleared circle. Had they been cultivated?

Hours went by as I stared out through the ports, at this fascinating and bewildering moonscape.

Finally I recalled the pictures that my uncle had requested me to make. For two or three hours I was busy with the cameras. I made exposures in all directions, with ordinary and telescopic lenses, I photographed the scene with colour filters. And finally I made motion pictures, swinging the camera to take a panoramic view.

It was almost sunset when I had done. It seemed strange that the day was passing so swiftly, until I looked at the chronometer, found that it was not keeping pace with the sun, and decided that the period of rotation must be rather less than twenty-four hours. I later found it to be about eighteen hours, divided into days and nights of very nearly equal length.

Darkness came very swiftly after sunset, due to the comparatively small size and quick rotation of the moon. The stars burst out splendidly through the clear air, burning in constellations utterly strange.

A heavy dew was soon obscuring the ports. As I later discovered, clouds almost never formed in this light atmosphere. Nearly the entire precipitation was in the form of dew, which, however, was amazingly abundant. The tiny droplets on the glass were soon running in streams.

After a few hours, a huge and glorious snow-white sphere rose in the east. The earth. Wondrous in size and brilliance.

The weird jungle was visible in its silvery radiance almost as in daylight.

Suddenly I realized that I was tired, and very sleepy. The anxiety and prolonged nervous strain of the landing had been exhausting. I threw myself down upon the reclining chair, and fell into immediate oblivion.

The white sun was high when I woke. I found myself refreshed. Keenly hungry. And conscious of a great need for physical exercise. Accustomed to an active life, I had been shut up in that little round room for seven days. I felt that I must move, breathe fresh air.

Could I leave the machine?

My uncle had told me that it would be impossible, because of lack of atmosphere. But there was plainly air about me, on this young moon. Would it be breathable?

I pondered the question. The moon, I knew, was formed of materials thrown off the cooling earth. Then should its atmosphere not contain the same elements as that of earth?

I decided to try it. Open the door slightly, and sniff experimentally. Close it immediately if there seemed anything wrong.

I loosened the screws that held the heavy door, tried to pull it open. It seemed fastened immovably. In vain I tugged at it, looked to see if I had left a screw, or if something was amiss with the hinges. It refused to budge.

For minutes I was baffled. The explanation came to me suddenly. The pressure of the atmosphere outside was much less than that within the machine. Since the door opened inward, it was the unbalanced pressure upon it that held it.

I found the valve which was to be opened to free the chamber of any dangerous excess of oxygen that might escape, and spun it open. The air hissed out noisily.

I sat down in the chair to wait. At first I felt no symptoms of the lessening pressure. Then I was conscious of a sensation of lightness, of exhilaration. I noticed that I was breathing faster. My temples throbbed. For a few minutes I felt a dull ache in my lungs.

But the sensations did not become unduly alarming, and I left the valve open. The hissing sound gradually decreased, and finally died away completely.

I rose and went to the door, feeling a painful shortness of the breath as I moved. The heavy door came open quite easily now. I sniffed the air outside. It bore a strange, heavy, unfamiliar fragrance which must have been carried from the jungle in the valley. And I found it oddly stimulating – it must have been richer in oxygen than the air in the machine.

With the door flung wide, I breathed deeply of it.

At first I had thought merely of strolling up and down for a while, in the moss outside the machine. But now I decided, quite suddenly, to hike to the lower edge of the green-carpeted plateau, perhaps a mile away, and look at the edge of the jungle.

I looked about for equipment that I should take, got together a few items. A light camera, in case I should see something worth taking. The binoculars. A vacuum bottle full of water, and a little food, so that I should not have to hasten back to eat.

And finally I took down the automatic pistol on the wall, a .45 Colt. It must have been included with the machine's equipment merely as a way of merciful escape, in case some failure made life in the little round compartment unendurable. There was only one box of ammunition. Fifty cartridges. I loaded the weapon, and slipped the remainder into my pocket.

Gathering up the other articles, I scrambled through the oval door, and stood upon the rim of the lower copper disc, drawing the door to behind me, and fastening it.

And stepped off, upon the moon.

The thick, fibrous moss yielded under my foot, surprisingly. I stumbled, fell into its soft green pile. And in scrambling to my feet, I forgot the lesser gravity of the moon, threw myself into the air, tumbling once more into the yielding moss.

In a few mintues I had mastered the art of walking under the new conditions, so that I could stride along with some confidence, going clear of the ground at every step, as if I had worn seven-league boots. Once I essayed a leap. It carried me twenty feet into the air, and twice as far forward. It seemed that I hung in the air an unconscionable time, and floated down very slowly. But I was helpless, aloft, sprawling about, unable to get my feet beneath me. I came down on my shoulder, and must have been painfully bruised had it not been for the thick moss.

I realized that my strength upon the moon was quite out of proportion to my weight. I had muscles developed to handle a mass of 180 pounds. Here my weight was only 30 pounds. It would be some time, I supposed, before I could learn the exact force required to produce the result desired. Actually, I found myself adapted to these new conditions in a surprisingly short space of time.

For a time I was conscious of shortness of the breath, especially after violent exertion. But soon I was accustomed to the lighter air as well as the lesser gravitation.

In half an hour I had arrived at the edge of the red plateau. A steep slope fell before me to the edge of the jungle, perhaps two-thirds of a mile farther below. A slope carpeted with the thick fibre of the green moss.

A weird scene. Clear cerulean sky, darkly, richly blue. Huge white globe of the hot earth setting beyond the farther range of green mountains. The wide valley, with the broad silvery stream, winding among golden forests, and patches of green. The purple balloons floating here and yon, huge spheres swaying on the red cables that anchored them above the jungle.

I seated myself on the moss, where I could overlook that valley of eldritch wonder. I remained there for some time, staring out across it, while I ate most of the food that I had brought, and half-emptied the bottle of water.

Then I decided to descend to the edge of the jungle.

The sun was just at the meridian – the whole of the short afternoon, four hours and a half, was yet before me. I had ample time, I thought, to go down the slope to the edge of the jungle and return before the sudden nightfall.

I had no fear of getting lost. The glittering armour of the machine was visible over the whole plateau. And the jagged triple peak to the northward of it was a landmark which should be visible over the whole region. There should be no difficulty about return.

Nor, while I realized that the jungle might hid hostile life, did I fear attack. I intended to be cautious, and not to penetrate beyond the edge of the jungle. I had the automatic, which, I was sure, gave me greater power of destruction than any other animal on the planet. Finally in case of difficulty, I could rely upon the superior strength of my muscles, which must be far stronger, in proportion to my weight, than those of native creatures.

I found progress easy on the long, mossy incline. My skill at travelling under lunar conditions of gravity was increasing with practice: I found a way of moving by deliberate, measured leaps, each carrying me twenty feet or more.

In a few minutes I found myself approaching the edge of the jungle. But that was not so sharp a line as it had appeared from above. The first vegetation other than the moss was scattered clumps of a plant resembling the cactus of my native Southwest.

Thick, fleshy discs growing one upon another, edge to edge. They were not green, however, but of a curious pink, flesh-like colour. They bore no thorns, but were studded with little black protuberances or knobs, of doubtful function. The plants I first approached were small and appeared stunted. The lower clumps seemed larger, and more thickly spaced.

I paused to examine one. Walked around it curiously. Photographed it from several angles. Then I ventured to touch it with my foot. Several of the little black knobs broke – they proved to be thin-walled vesicles, containing a black liquid. An overpowering and extremely unpleasant odour assailed me, and I retreated hastily.

A hundred yards farther on, I came upon the green creepers. Thick stems coiled like endless serpents over the ground, with innumerable fronds rising from them, terminating in feathery sprays of green. Here and there were huge white blooms, nearly six feet across, resembling great bells of burnished silver. From them, evidently, came the heavy perfume that I had noticed upon opening the door of the machine.

The creepers formed an unbroken mass of green, several feet deep. It would have been impossible to penetrate it without crushing the delicate foliage. I decided to go no farther in that direction. The creeper might have such means of protection as the malodorous sacs of the fleshy plants above. Or dangerous creatures, counterparts of terrene snakes, might lie concealed beneath the dense foliage.

For some distance I followed along the edge of the mass of creepers, pausing at intervals to make photographs. I was approaching a thicket or forest of the yellow scrub. A wall of inch-thick stems, each armed at intervals of a few inches with dagger-like thorns, all interwoven. A hundred feet high, I estimated. Interlaced so closely that a rat would have had difficulty in moving through it, without impaling himself upon a needle-sharp spike.

Then I paused to watch one of the purple balloons, which

seemed swaying toward me, increasing the length of the red anchor-cable which held it to the jungle behind. A strange thing, that huge purple sphere, tugging at the thin scarlet cable that held it. Tugging almost like a thing alive, I thought.

Several times I photographed it, but its distance was so great that I feared none of the images would be satisfactory. It seemed to be moving toward me, perhaps carried by some breeze that did not reach the ground. Perhaps, I thought, it would soon be near enough for a good picture.

IV

THE BALLOON MENACE

I studied it closely, trying to see if it had an intelligent pilot or occupant. But I was unable to settle the point. There was certainly no basket. But black arms or levers seemed to project in a cluster, from its lowest part, to manipulate the cables.

Nearly an hour, I waited, watching it. It moved much closer during that time; until, in fact, it was almost directly overhead, and only a few hundred feet high. The red cable slanted from it back into the jungle. It seemed to be loose, dragging.

At last I got a picture that satisfied me. I decided to go on and examine the tangle of yellow thorn-brush or scrub at closer range.

I had taken my eyes from the purple balloon, and turned to walk away, when it struck.

A red rope whipped about me.

The first I knew, it was already about my shoulders. Its end seemed to be weighted, for it whirled about my body several times, wrapping me in sticky coils.

The cable was about half an inch in diameter and made of many smaller crimson strands, fastened together with the adhesive stuff that covered it. I recall its appearance very vividly, even the odd, pungent, disagreeable odour of it.

Half a dozen coils of the red cable had whipped about me before I realized that anything was amiss. Then it tightened suddenly, dragging me across the red moss upon which I had been standing. Toward the edge of the jungle.

Looking up in horror, I saw that the rope had been thrown from the purple balloon I had been watching. Now the black arms that I had seen were working swiftly, coiling it up again – with me caught neatly on the end.

The great sphere was drawn down a little, as my weight came upon it. It seemed to swell. Then, having been dragged along until I was directly beneath it, I was lifted clear of the ground.

I was filled with unutterable terror. I was panting, my heart was beating swiftly. And I felt endowed with terrific strength. Furiously I writhed in my gluey bonds, struggled with the strength of desperation to break the red strands.

But the web had been spun to hold just such frightened, struggling animals as myself. It did not break.

Back and forth I swung over the jungle, like a pendulum. With a constantly quickening arc! For the cable was being drawn up. Once more I looked upward, and saw a sight to freeze me in dreadful stupefaction of horror.

The whole balloon was a living thing!

I saw its two black and terrible eyes, aflame with hot evil, staring at me from many bright facets. The black limbs I had seen were its legs, growing in a cluster at the bottom of its body – now furiously busy coiling up the cable that it had spun, spider-like, to catch me. I saw long jaws waiting, black and hideously fanged, drooling foul saliva. And a rapier-thin pointed snout, that must be meant for piercing, sucking body juices.

The huge purple sphere was a thin-walled, muscular sac, which must have been filled with some light gas, probably hydrogen, generated in the body of the creature. The amazing being floated above the jungle, out of harm's way, riding free on the wind, or anchored with its red web, lassoing its prey and hauling it up to feast hideously in the air.

For a moment I was petrified, dazed and helpless with the new horror of that thin snout, with black-fanged jaws behind it.

Then fear bred superhuman strength in me. I got my arms free, dragging them from beneath the sticky coils. I reached above my head, seized the red cable in both hands, tried to break it between them.

It refused to part, despite my fiercest efforts.

Only then did I recall the pistol in my pocket. If I could reach it in time, I might be able to kill the monster. And the gas should escape through the riddled sac, letting me back to the surface. I was already so high that the fall would have been dangerous, had I succeeded in my desperate effort to break the web.

The viscid stuff on the cable clung to my hands. It took all my strength to tear them loose. But at last they were free, and I fumbled desperately for the gun.

A red strand was across the pocket in which I had the weapon. I tore at it. It required every ounce of my strength to slip it upward. And it adhered to my fingers again. I wrenched them loose, snatched out the automatic. It touched the gluey rope, stuck fast. I dragged it free, moved the safety catch with sticky fingers, raised it above my head.

Though it had been seconds only since I was snatched up, already I had been lifted midway to the dreadful living balloon. I glanced downward. The distance was appalling. I noticed that the balloon was still drifting, so that I hung over a thicket of the yellow scrub.

Then I began shooting at the monster. It was difficult to aim, because of the regular jerks as the ugly black limbs hauled on the cable. I held the gun with both hands and fired deliberately, very carefully.

The first show seemed to have no effect.

At the second, I heard a shrill, deafening scream. And I saw that one of the black limbs was hanging limp.

I shot at the black, many-faceted eyes. Though I had no knowledge of the creature's anatomy, I supposed that its highest nervous centres should be near them.

The third shot hit one of them. A great blob of transparent jelly burst through the faceted surface, hung pendulous. The thing screamed horribly again. The black arms worked furiously, hauling me up.

I felt a violent upward jerk, stronger than the regular pulls that had been raising me. In a moment I saw the reason. The creature had released the long anchor cable, which had held it to the jungle. We were plunging upward. The moon was spinning away below.

The next shot seemed to take no effect. But at the fifth, the black limbs twitched convulsively. I am sure that the creature died almost at once. The limbs ceased to haul upon the cable, hung still. But I fired the two cartridges remaining in the gun.

That was the beginning of a mad aerial voyage.

The balloon shot upward, when the anchor cable was dropped. And after it was dead, the muscular sac seemed to relax, expand, so that it rose still faster.

Within a few minutes I must have been two miles above the surface. A vast area was visible beneath me; the convexity of the moon's surface, which, of course, is much greater than that of the earth's, was quite apparent.

The great valley lay below, between the green mountain ranges. Splotched with blue and yellow. The white river twisting along it, wide and silvery. I could see into other misty valleys beyond the green ranges, and on the curving horizon were more hills, dim and black in the distance.

The plateau upon which I had landed was like a green-covered table, many thousands of feet below. I could distinguish upon it a tiny bright disc, which I knew was the machine that I had left so unwisely.

Though there had been little wind at the surface, it seemed that I rose into a stratum of air, which was moving quite rapidly into the northwest. I was carried swiftly along; the floor of the great valley glided back beneath me. In a few minutes the machine was lost to view.

I was, of course, rendered desperate at being swept away from the machine. I kept myself oriented, and tried to watch the landmarks that passed beneath me. It was fortunate, I thought, that the wind was driving me up the valley, instead of across the red ranges. I might be able to return to the machine by following down the great river, until the triple peak, near which I had left the machine, came into view. Despair came over me, however, at the realization that I was not likely to be able to traverse so vast a stretch of the unknown jungles of this world, without my ignorance of its perils leading me into some fatal blunder.

I thought of climbing the web to that monstrous body, and trying to make a great rent in the purple sac, so that I should fall more swiftly. But I could only have succeeded in entangling myself more thoroughly in the adhesive coils. And I dismissed the scheme when I realized that if I fell too rapidly, I might be killed upon striking the surface.

After the first few minutes of the flight, I could see that the balloon was sinking slowly, as the gas escaped through the bullet holes in the muscular sac. I could only wait, and fix in my mind the route that I must follow back to the machine.

The wind bore me so swiftly along that within an hour the triple peak that I watched had dropped below the curved horizon. But still I was above the great valley, so that I should be able to find my way back by following the river. I wondered if I could build a raft, and float down with the current.

The balloon was carried along less rapidly as it approached the surface. But, as I neared the jungle, it was evident that it still drifted at considerable speed.

Hanging helpless in the end of the red web, I anxiously scanned the jungle into which I was descending. Like that which I had first seen, it was of dense tangles of the thorny yellow scrub, broken with areas covered largely with the luxuriant green creeper.

Never would I be able to extricate myself alive, I knew, if I had the misfortune to fall in the thorn brush. And another danger occurred to me. Even if I first touched ground in an open space, the balloon, if the wind continued to blow, would drag me into the spiky scrub before I could tear myself free of the web.

Could I cut myself free, within a safe distance of the ground, and let the balloon go on without me? It seemed that only thus could I escape being dragged to death. I knew that I could survive a fall from a considerable height, since the moon's acceleration of gravity is only about two feet per second – if only I could land on open ground.

But how could I cut the web? I was without a knife. I thought madly of attempting to bite it in two, realized that that would be as hopeless as attempting to bite through a manila rope.

But I still had the pistol. If I should place the muzzle against the cable and fire, the bullet should cut it.

I reached into my pocket again, past the adhesive coil, and found two cartridges. Though they clung to my sticky fingers, I got them at last into the magazine, and worked the action to throw one into the chamber.

By the time I had finished loading, I was low over an apparently endless jungle of the yellow thorns. Swaying on the end of the web, I was swept along over the spiky scrub, dropping swiftly. At last I could see the edge, and a green patch of the great creepers. For a time I hoped that I would be carried clear of the thorns.

Then they seemed suddenly to leap at me. I threw up my arms to shelter my face, still clinging fiercely to the pistol.

In an instant, I was being dragged through the cruel yellow spikes. There was a sharp, dry, crackling sound, as they broke beneath my weight. A thousand sharp, poisoned bayonets scratched at me, stabbed, cut.

Intolerable agony racked me. I screamed. The razor-sharp spikes were tipped with poison, so that the slightest scratch burned like liquid flame. And many of the stabbing points went deep.

It seems that I struck near the edge of the thicket. For a moment I hung there in the thorns. Then, as a harder puff of wind struck it, the balloon leaped into the air, dragging me free. I swung up like a pendulum. And down again, beyond the thorny scrub – over a strip of bare sand beside the thicket.

Bleeding rapidly from my cuts, and suffering unendurable pain from the poison in my wounds, I realized that I could not long remain conscious.

Moving in a haze of agony, I seized the red cable with one hand, put the muzzle of the automatic against it, pulled the trigger. The report was crashing, stunning. My right hand, holding the gun, was flung back by the recoil – I should have lost the weapon had it not been glued to my fingers. The cable was jerked with terrific force, almost breaking my left hand, with which I held it.

And it parted! I plunged downward, sprawled on the sand.

For a few minutes I remained conscious as I lay there on the hard, cold sand – the first soil, I recall thinking vaguely in my agony, that I had seen not covered with vegetation.

The clothing had been half stripped from my tortured body by the thorns. I was bleeding freely from several deeper cuts – I remember how dark the blood was, sinking into the white sand.

All my body throbbed with insufferable pain, from the poison in my wounds. As if I had been plunged into a sea of flame. Only my face had been spared.

Weakly, dizzy with pain, I tried to stagger to my feet. But

a coil of the red web still clung about my legs. It tripped me, and I fell forward again, upon the white sand.

Fell into bitter despair. Into blind, hopeless rage at my inane lack of caution in leaving the machine. At my fool-hardiness in venturing into the edge of the jungle. Fell into gentle oblivion. . . .

A curious sound drew me back into wakefulness. A thin, high-pitched piping, pleasantly melodious. The musical notes beat insistently upon my brain, evidently originating quite near me.

On first awakening, I was aware of no bodily sensation. My mind was peculiarly dull and slow. I was unable to recall where I was. My first impression was that I was lying in bed in my old rooming place at Midland and that my alarm clock was ringing. But soon I realized that the liquid piping notes that had disturbed me came from no alarm.

I forced open heavy eyes. What startling nightmare was this? A tangle of green creepers, incredibly profuse. A wall of yellow thorns. A scarlet mountain beyond. And purple balloons floating in a rich blue sky.

I tried to sit up. My body burst into screaming agony when I moved. And I sank back. My skin was stiff with dry blood. The deeper wounds were aching. And the poison from the thorns seemed to have stiffened my muscles, so that the slightest motion brought exquisite pain.

The melodious pipings had been abruptly silenced at my movement. But now they rose again. Behind me. I tried to turn my head.

Recollection was returning swiftly. My uncle's telegram. The flight through space and time. My expedition to the jungle's edge, and its horrible sequel. I still lay where I had fallen, on the bare sand below the spiky scrub.

I groaned despite myself, with the pain of my stiff body. The thin musical notes stopped again. And the thing that had voiced them glided around before me, so that I could see it.

A strange and wonderful being.

Its body was slender, flexible as an eel. Perhaps five feet long, it was little thicker than my upper arm. Soft, short golden down or fur covered it. Part of it was coiled on the sand; its head was lifted two or three feet.

A small head, not much larger than my fist. A tiny mouth, with curved lips full and red as a woman's. And large eyes, dark and intelligent. They were deeply violet, almost luminous. Somehow they looked human, perhaps only because they mirrored the human qualities of curiosity and pity.

Aside from red mouth and dark eyes, the head had no human features. Golden down covered it. On the crown was a plume or crest of brilliant blue. But strange as it was, it possessed a certain beauty. A beauty of exquisite proportion, of smooth curves.

Curious wing-like appendages or mantles grew from the sides of the sleek, golden body, just below the head. Now they were stiffened, extended as if for flight. They were very white, of thin membrane. Their snowy surfaces were finely veined with scarlet.

Other than these white, membranous mantles, the creature had no limbs. Slim, long, pliant body, covered with golden fur. Small, delicate head, with red mouth and warm dark eyes, crested with blue. And delicate wings thrust out from its sides.

I stared at it.

Even at first sight, I did not fear it, though I was helpless. It seemed to have a magnetic power that filled me with quiet confidence, assured me that it meant only good.

The lips pursed themselves. And the thin, musical piping sound came from them again. Was the thing speaking to me? I uttered the first phrase that entered my mind, 'Hello. Who are we, anyhow?'

V

THE MOTHER

The thing glided toward me swiftly, its smooth round golden body leaving a little twisting track in the white sand. It lowered its head a little. And it laid one of the white mantles across my forehead.

The strange red-veined membrance was soft, yet there was an odd firmness in its pressure against my skin. A vital warmth seemed to come from it – it was vibrant with energy, with life.

The pipings came again. And they seemed to stir vague

148

response in my mind, to call dim thoughts into being. As the same sounds were repeated again and again, definite questions formed in my mind.

'What are you? How did you come here?'

Through some strange telepathy induced by the pressure of the mantle upon my head, I was grasping the thought in the piping words.

It was a little time before I was sufficiently recovered from my astonishment to speak. Then I replied slowly, phrasing my expressions carefully, and uttering them as distinctly as I could.

'I am a native of Earth. Of the great white globe you can see in the sky. I came here in a machine which moves through space and time. I left it, and was caught and jerked up into the air by one of those purple, floating things. I broke the web, and fell here. My body was so torn by the thorns that I cannot move.'

The thing piped again. A single quavering note. It was repeated until its meaning formed in my mind.

'I understand.'

'Who are you?' I ventured.

I got the meaning of the reply, as it was being piped for the third time. 'I am the Mother. The Eternal Ones, who destroyed my people, pursue me. To escape them, I am going to the sea.'

And the thin, musical tones came again. This time I understood them more easily.

'Your body seems slow to heal its hurts. Your mental force is feeble. May I aid you?'

'Of course,' I said. 'Anything you can do –'

'Lie still. Trust me. Do not resist. You must sleep.' When the meaning of the notes came to me, I relaxed upon the sand, closed my eyes.

I could feel the warm, vibrant pressure of the mantle on my forehead. Vital, throbbing force seemed pulsing into me through it. I felt no fear, despite the strangeness of my situation. A living wave of confidence came over me. Serene trust in the power of this being. I felt a command to sleep. I did not resist it; a strong tide of vital energy swept me into oblivion.

It seemed but an instant later, though it must have been many hours, when an insistent voice called me back from sleep.

Vitality filled me. Even before I opened my eyes, I was conscious of a new and abounding physical vigour, of perfect health; I was bubbling with energy and high spirits, And I knew, by the complete absence of bodily pain, that my wounds were completely healed.

I opened my lids, saw the amazing creature that had called itself the Mother. Its smooth golden body coiled beside me on the sand. Its large, clear eyes watching me intently, with kind sympathy.

Abruptly I sat up. My limbs were stiff no longer. My body was still caked with dried blood, clothed in my tattered garments; the sticky scarlet coils of the web were still around me. But my ragged wounds were closed. Only white scars showed where they had been.

'Why, I'm well!' I told the mother, thankfully. 'How'd you do it?'

The strange being piped melodiously, and I grasped the meaning almost at once. 'My vital force is stronger than your own. I merely lent you energy.'

I began tearing at the coils of the crimson web about me. Their viscid covering seemed to have dried a little; otherwise I might never have got them off. After a moment the Mother glided forward and helped.

It used the white, membranous appendages like hands. Though they appeared quite frail, they seemed able to grasp the red cable powerfully when they were folded about it.

In a few minutes I was on my feet.

Again the Mother piped at me. I failed to understand, though vague images were summoned to my mind. I knelt down again on the sand, and the being glided toward me, pressed the white, red-veined mantle once more against my forehead. An amazing organ, that mantle, so delicately beautiful. So strong of grasp when used as a hand. And useful, as I was to learn, as an organ of some strange sense.

The meanings of the pipings came to me clearly now, with the warm, vibrant mantle touching my head.

'Adventurer, tell me more of your world, and how you came here. My people are old, and I have vital powers beyond your own. But we have never been able to go beyond the atmosphere of our planet. Even the Eternal Ones, with all their machines, have never been able to bridge the gulf of space. And it has been thought that the primary planet from which you say you come is yet too hot for the development of life.'

For many hours we talked, I in my natural voice, the Mother in those weirdly melodious pipings. At first the transference of thought by the telepathy which the wonderful mantle made possible was slow and awkward. I, especially, had trouble in receiving, and had many times to ask the Mother to repeat a complex thought. But facility increased with practice, and I at last was able to understand, quite readily, even when the white membrane did not touch me.

The sun had been low when I woke. It set, and the dew fell upon us. We talked on in the darkness. And the earth rose, illuminating the jungle with argent glory. Still we talked, until it was day again. For a time the air was quite cold. Wet with the abundant dew, I felt chilled, and shivered.

But the Mother touched me again with the white membrane. Quick, throbbing warmth seemed to flow from it into my body, and I felt cold no longer.

I told much of the world that I had left, and of my own insignificant life upon it. Told of the machine. Of the voyage across space, and back through æons of time, to this young moon.

And the Mother told he of her life, and of her lost people.

She had been the leader of a community of beings that had lived on the highlands, near the source of the great river that I had seen, A community in some respects resembling those of ants or bees upon the earth. It had contained thousands of neuter beings, imperfectly developed females, workers. And herself, the only member capable of reproduction. She was now the sole survivor of that community.

It seemed that her race was very old, and had developed a high civilization. The Mother admitted that her people had had no machines or buildings of any kind. She declared that such things were marks of barbarism, and that her own culture was superior to mine.

'Once we had machines,' she told me. 'My ancient mothers lived in shells of metal and wood, such as you describe. And constructed machines to aid and protect their weak and inefficient bodies.

'But the machines tended to weaken their poor bodies still further. Their limbs atrophied, perished from lack of use. Even their brains were injured, for they lived an easy life, depending upon machines for existence, facing no new problems.

'Some of my people awoke to the danger. They left the cities, and returned to the forest and the sea, to live sternly, to depend upon their own minds and their own bodies, to remain living things, and not grow into cold machines.

'The mothers divided. And my people were those that returned to the forest.'

'And what,' I asked, 'of those that remained in the city, that kept the machines?'

'They became the Eternal Ones – my enemies.

'Generation upon generation their bodies wasted away. Until they were no longer natural animals. They became mere brains, with eyes and feeble tentacles. In place of bodies, they use machines. Living brains, with bodies of metal.

'Too weak, they became, to reproduce their kind. So they sought immortality, with their mechanical science. And still some of them live on, in their ugly city of metal – though for ages no young have been born among them. The Eternal Ones. But at last they die, because that is the way of life. Even with all their knowledge they cannot live forever. One by one, they fall. Their strange machines are still, with rotting brains in the cases.

'And the few thousands that live attacked my people. They planned to take the Mothers. To change their offspring with their hideous arts, and make of them new brains for the machines.

'The Mothers were many, when the war began. And my people a thousand times more. Now only I remain. But it was no easy victory for the Eternal Ones. My people fought bravely. Many an ancient brain they killed. But the Eternal Onces had great engines of war, that we could not escape, nor destroy with our vital energy.

'All the Mothers save myself were taken. And all destroyed themselves, rather than have their children made into living machines.

'I alone escaped. Because my people sacrificed their lives for me. In my body are the seed of a new race. I seek a home for my children. I have left our old land on the shores of the lake, and I am going down to the sea. There we shall be far from the Eternal Land. And perhaps our enemies will never find us.

'But the Eternal Ones know I have escaped. They are hunting me. Hunting me with all their strange machines.'

When day came, I felt very hungry. What was I to do for food in this weird jungle? Even if I could find fruits or nuts, how could I tell whether they were poisonous? I mentioned my hunger.

'Come,' the Mother piped.

She glided away across the white sand, with easy, sinuous grace. Very beautiful, she was. Slim body, smooth, rounded. Compactly trim. The golden down was bright in the sunlight; sapphire rays played over the blue plume upon her head. The wondrous, red-veined mantles at her sides shone brilliantly.

Regarding her strange beauty, I stood still for a moment, and then moved after her slowly, absently.

She turned back suddenly, with something like humour flashing in her great dark violet eyes.

'Is your great body so slow you cannot keep up with me?' she piped, almost derisively. 'Shall I carry you?' Her eyes were mocking.

For answer I crouched, leaped into the air. My wild spring carried me a score of feet above her, and beyond. I had the misfortune to come down head first upon the sand, though I received no injury.

I saw laughter in her eyes, as she glided swiftly to me, and grasped my arm with one of the white mantles to assist me to my feet.

'You could travel splendidly if there were two of you, one to help the other out of the thorns,' she said quaintly.

A little embarrassed by her mockery, I followed meekly.

We reached a mass of the green creeper. Without hesitation, she pushed on through the feathery foliage. I broke through behind her. She led the way to one of the huge white flowers, bent it toward her, and crept into it like a golden bee.

In a moment she emerged with mantles cupped up to hold a good quantity of white, crystalline powder which she had scraped from the inside of the huge calyx.

She made me hold my hands, and dropped part of the powder into them. She lifted what she had left, upon the other mantle, and began delicately licking at it with her lips.

I tasted it. It was sweet, with a peculiar, though not at all unpleasant, acid flavour. It formed a sort of gum as it was wetted in my mouth, and this softened and dissolved as I continued to chew. I took a larger bite, and soon finished all the Mother had given me. We visited another bloom. This time I reached in, and scraped out the powder with my own hand. (The crystals must have been formed for the same purpose as the nectar in terrene flowers – to attract raiders, which carry the pollen.)

I divided my booty with the Mother. She accepted but little, and I found enough of the sweetish powder in the calyx to satisfy my own hunger.

'Now I must go on down to the sea,' she piped. 'Too long already have I delayed with you. For I carry the seed of my race; I must not neglect the great work that has fallen upon me.

'But I was glad to know of your strange planet. And it is good to be with an intelligent being again, when I had been so long alone. I wish I could stay longer with you. But my wishes are not my master.'

Thoughts of parting from her were oddly disturbing. My feeling for her was partly gratitude for saving my life and partly something else. A sense of comradeship. We were companion adventurers in this weird and lonely jungle. Solitude and my human desire for society of any sort drew me toward her.

Then came an idea. She was going down the valley to the sea. And my way led in the same direction, until I could see the triple peak that marked the location of the machine.

'May I travel with you,' I asked her,' 'until we reach the mountain where I left the machine in which I came to your world?'

The Mother looked at me with fine dark eyes. And glided suddenly nearer. A white membranous mantle folded about my hand, with warm pressure.

'I am glad you wish to go with me,' she piped. 'But you must think of the danger. Remember that I am hunted by the Eternal Ones. They will doubtless destroy you if they find us together.'

'I have a weapon,' I said, 'I'll put up a scrap for you, if we get in a tight place. And besides, I'd very likely be killed, in one way or another, if I tried to travel alone.'

'Let us go, Adventurer.'

Thus it was decided.

I had dropped the camera, the binoculars, and the vacuum

bottle when the balloon creature jerked me into the air. They were lost in the jungle. But I still had the automatic. It had remained in my hand – stuck to it, in fact – when I fell upon the sand. I carried it with me.

The Mother objected to the weapon. Because it was a machine, and machines weakened all that used them. But I insisted that we should have to fight machines, if the Eternal Ones caught us, and that fire could be best fought with fire. She yielded gracefully.

'But my vital force will prove stronger than your rude slaying machine, Adventurer,' she maintained.

We set out almost immediately. She glided off along the strip of bare sand beside the wall of thorny yellow scrub. And began my instruction in the ways of life upon the moon, by informing me that there was always such a clear zone about a thicket of the thorn brush, because its roots generated a poison in the soil which prevented the growth of other vegetation near them.

When we had travelled two or three miles, we came to a crystal pool, where the abundant dew had collected at the bottom of a bare, rocky slope. We drank there. Then the Mother plunged into it joyously. With white mantles folded tight against her sides, she flashed through the water like a golden eel. I was glad to remove my own garments, and wash the grime and dried blood from my body.

I was donning my tattered clothing again, and the Mother was lying beside me, at the edge of the pool, with eyes closed, drying her golden fur in the sunshine, when I saw the ghostly bars.

Seven thin upright pillars of light, ringed about us. Straight bars of pale white radiance. They stood like phantom columns about us, enclosing a space ten yards across. They were not above two inches in diameter. And they were quite transparent, so I could see the green jungle and the yellow wall of thorn bush quite plainly through them.

I was not particularly alarmed. In fact, I thought the ghostly pillars only some trick of my vision. I rubbed my eyes, and said rather carelessly to the Mother:

'Are the spirits building a fence around us? Or is it just my eyes?'

She lifted her golden, blue-crested head quickly. Her violet eyes went wide. I saw alarm in them. Terror. And she moved

with astonishing speed. Drew her slender length into a coil.
Leaped. And seized my shoulders as she leaped, with one of
her mantles.

She jerked me between two of those strange columns of
motionless light, out of the area they enclosed.

I fell on the sand, got quickly to my feet.

'What –' I began.

'The Eternal Ones,' her sweet, whistling tones came swiftly.
'They have found me. Even here, they reach me with their
evil power. We must go on, quickly.'

She glided swiftly away. Still buttoning my clothing, I
followed, keeping pace with her easily, with my regular leaps
of half a dozen yards. Followed, wondering vainly what
danger there might have been in the pillars of ghostly light.

VI

PURSUIT!

We skirted a continuous wall of the spiky yellow scrub.

The strip of clear ground we followed was usually fifty to
one hundred yards wide. The mass of yellow thorn brush, the
poison from whose roots had killed the vegetation here, rose
dense and impenetrable to our right. To the left of our open
way limitless stretches covered with the green creeper. Un-
dulating seas of feathery emerald foliage. Scattered with huge
white blooms. Broken, here and there, with strange plants of
various kinds. Beyond were other clumps of the yellow scrub.
A red mountain wall rose in the distance. Huge purple
balloons swayed here and there upon this weird, sunlit moonscape, anchored with their red cables.

I suppose we followed that open strip for ten miles. I was
beginning to breathe heavily, as violent exercise always made
me do in the moon's light atmosphere. The Mother showed no
fatigue.

Abruptly she paused ahead of me, and glided into a sort
of tunnel through the forest of thorns. A passage five feet
wide and six feet high, with the yellow spokes arching over
it. The floor was worn smooth, hard-packed as if by constant

use. It seemed almost perfectly straight, for I could see down it for a considerable distance. Twilight filled it, filtering down through the unbroken mass of cruel bayonets above.

'I am not eager to use this path,' the Mother told me. 'For they who made it are hostile things. And though not very intelligent, they are able to resist my vital force, so that I cannot control them. We shall be helpless if they discover us.

'But there is no other way. We must cross this forest of thorns. And I am glad to be out of sight in this tunnel. Perhaps the Eternal Ones will lose us again. We must hasten, and hope that we encounter no rightful user of the path. If one appears, we must hide.'

I was placed immediately at a disadvantage upon entering the tunnel, for I could no longer take the long leaps by which I had been travelling. My pace became a sort of trot. I had to hold my head down, to save it from the poisoned thorns above.

The Mother glided easily before me, to my relief not in such haste as before. Slender and strong and trimly beautiful – for all her strangeness. I was glad she had let me come with her. Even if peril threatened.

I found breath for speech.

'Those ghostly bars,' I panted, 'What were they?'

'The Eternal Ones possess strange powers of science,' came the thin, whistling notes of her reply. 'Something like the television you told me of. But more highly developed. They were able to see us, back by the pool.

'And the shining bars were projected through space by their rays of force. They meant some harm to us. Just what, I do not know. It is apparently a new weapon, which they did not use in the war.'

We must have gone many miles through the tunnel. It had been almost perfectly straight. There had been no branches or cross passages. We had come through no open space. Roof and walls of yellow thorns had been unbroken. I was wondering what sort of creature it might be, that had made a path through the thorns so long and straight.

The Mother stopped suddenly, turned back to face me.

'One of the makers of the trail is approaching,' she piped. 'I feel it coming. Wait for me a bit.'

She sank in golden coils upon the trail. Her head was raised a little. The mantles were extended stiffly. Always before they had been white, except for their fine veining of red. But now soft, rosy colours flushed them. Her full red lips were parted a little, and her eyes had become strange, wide, staring. They seemed to look past me, to gaze upon scenes far off, invisible to ordinary sight.

For long seconds she remained motionless, violet eyes distant, staring.

Then she stirred abruptly. Rose upon tawny, golden coils. Alarm was in her great eyes, in her thin, melodious tones.

'The creature comes behind us. Upon this trail. We have scant time to reach the open. We must go swiftly.'

She waited for me to begin my stumbling run, glided easily beside me. I moved awkwardly. With only the moon's slight gravitational pull to hold me to the trail, I was in constant danger from the thorns.

For tortured hours, it seemed to me, we raced down the straight passage, through the unbroken forest of yellow thorns. My heart was labouring painfully; my breath came in short gasps of agony. My body was not equipped for such prolonged exertions in the light air.

The Mother, just ahead of me, glided along with effortless ease. I knew that she could easily have left me, had she wished.

At last I stumbled, fell headlong, and did not have energy to get at once to my feet. My lungs burned, my heart was a great ache. Sweat was pouring from me; my temples throbbed; and a red mist obscured my sight.

'Go – on,' I gasped, between panting breaths. 'I'll try – to stop – it.'

I fumbled weakly for my gun.

The Mother stopped, came back to me. Her piping notes were quick, insistent. 'Come. We are near the open now. And the thing is close. You must come!'

With a soft, flexible mantle she seized my arm. It seemed to me that a wave of new strength and energy came into me from it. At any rate, I staggered to my feet, lurched forward again. As I rose, I cast a glance backward.

A dark, indistinguishable shape was in view. So large that it filled almost the whole width of the tunnel. A dim circle of the pale light of the thorn forest showed around it.

I ran on ... on ... on.

My legs rose and fell, rose and fell, like the insensate levers of an automaton. I felt no sensation from them. Even my lungs had ceased to burn, since the Mother touched me. And my heart ached no longer. It seemed that I floated beside my body, and watched it run, run, run with the monotonously repeated movements of a machine.

My eyes were upon the Mother before me.

Gliding so swiftly through the twilight of the tunnel. Trim, round golden body. White mantles extended stiffly, wing-like, as if to help carry her. Delicate head raised, the blue plume upon it flashing.

I watched that blue plume as I ran. It danced mockingly before me, always retreating. Always just beyond my grasp. I followed it through the blinding mists of fatigue, when all the rest of the world melted into a grey-blue, streaked with bloody crimson.

I was astonished when we came out into the sunlight. A strip of sand below the yellow wall of thorns. Cool green foliage beyond, a sea of green. Sinister purple balloons above it, straining on crimson cables. Far off, a scarlet line of mountains, steep and rugged.

The Mother turned to the left.

I followed, automatically, mechanically. I was beyond feeling. I could see the bright moonscape, but it was strange no longer.

Even the threat of the purple balloons was remote, without consequence.

I do not know how far we ran, beside the forest of thorns, before the Mother turned again and led the way into a mass of creepers.

'Lie still,' she piped. 'The creature may not find us.'

Gratefully, I flung myself down in the delicate fronds. I lay flat, with my eyes closed, my breath coming in great, painful, sobbing gasps. The Mother folded my hand in her soft mantle again, and immediately, it seemed, I felt relief, though I still breathed heavily.

'Your reserve of vital energy is very low,' she commented.

I took the automatic from my pocket, examined it to see that it was ready for action. I had cleaned and loaded it before we started. I saw the Mother raising her blue-crested head cautiously. I got to my knees, peered back along the bare strip of sand, down which we had come.

I saw the thing advancing swiftly along the sand.

A sphere of bright crimson. Nearly five feet in diameter. It rolled along, following the way we had come.

'It has found us!' the Mother piped, very softly. 'And my vital power cannot reach through its armour. It will suck the fluids from our bodies.'

I looked down at her. She had drawn her slender body into a golden coil. Her head rose in the centre, and the mantles were outspread, pure white, veined with fine lines of scarlet, and frail as the petals of a lily. Her great dark eyes were grave and calm; there was no trace of panic in them.

I raised the automatic, determined to show no more fear than she, and to give my best to save her.

Now the scarlet globe was no more than fifty yards away. I could distinguish the individual scales of its armour, looking like plates of horn covered with ruby lacquer. No limbs or external appendages were visible then. But I saw dark ovals upon the shell, appearing at the top and seeming to drop down, as the thing rolled. I began shooting.

At such a distance there was no possibility of missing. I knelt in the leaves of the green creeper, and emptied the magazine into the globe.

It continued to roll on toward us, without change of speed. But a deep, angry drumming sound came from within it. A reverberating roar of astonishing volume. After a few moments, I heard it repeated from several points about us. Low and distant rumblings, almost like thunder.

In desperate haste, I was filling the clip with fresh cartridges. Before I could snap it back into the gun, the creature was upon us.

Until it stopped, it had presented a sphere of unbroken surface. But suddenly six long, glistening black tentacles reached out of it, one from each of the black ovals I had seen evenly spaced about the red shell. They were a dozen feet long, slender, covered with thin black skin corrugated with innumerable wrinkles, and glistening with tiny drops of moisture. At the base of each was a single, staring, black-lidded eye.

One of those black tentacles was thrust toward me. It reeked with an overpowering, fetid odour. At its extremity was a sharp, hooked claw, beside a black opening. I think the creature sucked its food through those hideous, retractable tentacles.

I got the loaded clip into the gun, hastily snapped a cartridge into the chamber. Shrinking back from the writing tentacular arm. I fired seven shots, as rapidly as I could press the trigger, into the black-lidded eye.

The deep drumming notes came from within the red shell again. The black tentacles writhed, thrashed about, and became suddenly stiff and rigid. The sound of it died to a curious rattle, and then ceased.

'You have killed it,' the Mother whistled musically. 'You use your machine well, and it is more powerful than I thought. Perhaps, after all, we may yet live.'

As if in ominous answer, a reverberating roll of distant drumming came from the tangle of yellow thorns. She listened, and the white mantles were stiffened in her alarm.

'But it has called to its kind. Soon many will be here. We must hasten away.'

Though I was still so tired that movement was torture, I rose and followed the Mother, as she glided on along the sand.

Only a moment did I pause to examine the very interesting creature I had killed. It seemed unique, both in shape and in means of locomotion. It must have developed the spherical shell of red armour through ages of life in the spiky scrub. By drawing its limbs inside, it was able to crash through the thorns without suffering any hurt. I supposed it contrived to roll along by some rhythmic muscular contraction, inside the shell – such movement being much easier on the moon than it would be on earth, because of the lesser gravity. Where it could not roll, it dragged or lifted itself with the long, muscular appendages that I have called tentacles.

Since we were in the open air again, I was able to resume my progression by deliberate, measured leaps, which carried me forward as fast as the Mother could move, and with much less effort than I had spent in running. I had a few moments of rest as I glided through the air between leaps, which compensated for the fiercer effort of each spring.

From time to time I looked back, nervously. At first I could see only the scarlet shell of the dead creature, there by the green vines where we had killed it. Always smaller, until it was hardly visible.

Then I saw other spheres. Emerging from the tangle of yellow thorn brush. Rolling along the strip of bare soil, to congregate about the dead thing. Finally I saw they had started in our direction, rolling along faster than we could move.

'They are coming,' I told the Mother. 'And more of them than I can kill.'

'They are implacable,' came her piping reply. 'When one of them sets out upon the trail of some luckless creature, it never stops until it has sucked the body fluids from it – or until it is dead.'

'Anything we can do?' I questioned.

'There is a rock ahead of us, beyond that thicket. A small hill, whose sides are so steep they will not be able to climb it. If we can reach it in time, we may be able to scramble to the top.

'It will be only temporary escape, since the creatures will never leave so long as we are alive upon it. But we shall delay our fate, at least – if we can reach it in time.'

Again I looked back. Our pursuers were rolling along like a group of red marbles, at the edge of the yellow forest. Gaining upon us – swiftly.

The Mother glided along more rapidly. The white mantles were stiffly extended from her golden sides, and aglow with rosy colours. The muscles beneath her furry skin rippled evenly, gracefully.

I increased the force of my own leaps.

We rounded an arm of the tangle of scrub, came in sight of the rock. A jutting mass of black granite. Its sides leaped up steep and bare from a mass of green creepers. Green moss crowned it. Thirty feet high it was. Perhaps a hundred in length.

Our pursuers were no longer merely marbles when we saw the rock. They had grown to the size of baseballs. Rolling swiftly after us.

The Mother glided on, a tireless strength in her graceful tawny body. And I leaped desperately, straining to drive myself as fast as possible.

We turned. Broke through the thick masses of verdure to the rock. Stood beneath its sheer wall, grim and black.

The red spheres were no more than a hundred yards behind. A sudden rumble of drums came from them, when we halted by the rock. I could see the dark ovals on their glistening red armour, that marked their eyes and the ends of their concealed tentacles.

'I can never climb that,' the Mother was piping.

'I can leap up!' I cried. 'Earth muscles. I'll carry you up.'

'Better that one should live than both of us die,' she said. 'I can delay them, until you reach the top.'

She started gliding back, toward the swiftly rolling spheres.

I bent, snatched her up.

It was the first time that I had felt her body. The golden fur was short, and very soft. The rounded body beneath it was firm, muscular, warm and vibrant. It throbbed with life. I felt that a strange sudden surge of energy was coming into me from contact with it.

I threw her quickly over my shoulder, ran forward a few steps, leaped desperately up at that sheer wall of black granite.

My own weight, on the moon, was only thirty pounds. The Mother, compact and strong though she was, weighed no more than a third as much. Combined, our weight was then some forty pounds. But, as she had realized, it was an apparently hopeless undertaking to attempt to hurl that mass to the top of the cliff before us.

At first I thought I should make it, as we soared swiftly up and up, toward the crown of red moss. Then I realized that we should strike the face of the cliff before we reached the top.

The face of the black rock was sheer. But my searching eyes caught a little projecting ledge. As we fell against the vertical cliff, my fingers caught that ledge. A moment of dreadful uncertainty, for the ledge was mossy, slippery.

VII

THE ETERNAL ONES FOLLOW!

My left hand slipped suddenly off. But the right held. I drew myself upward. The Mother slipped from my shoulder to the top of the rock. Grasped my left hand with one of the white mantles, drew me to safety.

Trembling from the strain of it, I got to my feet upon the soft scarlet moss, and surveyed our fortress. The moss-covered surface was almost level, a score of feet wide at the middle, where we stood, and a hundred in length. On all sides the walls were steep, though not everywhere so steep as where I had leaped up.

'Thank you, Adventurer,' the Mother whistled musically. 'You have saved my life, and the lives of all my people to come.'

'I was merely repaying a debt,' I told her.

We watched the red globes. Very soon they reached the foot of the cliff. The rumble of drums floated up from the group of them. And they scattered, surrounding the butte.

Presently we discovered that they were attempting to climb up. They were not strong enough to make the leap as I had done. But they were finding fissures and ledges upon which their long tentacles could find a grasp, drawing themselves up.

We patrolled the sides of the rock regularly, and I shot those which seemed to be making the best progress. I was able to aim carefully at an eye or the base of a tentacle. And usually a single shot was enough to send the climber rolling back down to the green jungle.

The view from our stronghold was magnificent. On one side was an endless wall of yellow scrub, with crimson mountains towering above it in the distance. On the other, the green tangle of the luxuriant creepers swept down to the wide silver river. Yellow and green mottled the slope that stretched up to scarlet hills beyond.

We held out for an entire day.

The sun sank beyond the red mountains when we had been upon the butte only an hour or two. A dark night would have terminated our adventures on the spot. But fortunately the huge white disc of the earth rose almost immediately after sunset, and gave sufficient light throughout the night to enable us to see the spheres that persisted in attempting to climb the walls of our fort.

It was late on the following afternoon that I used my last shot. I turned to the Mother with the news that I could no longer keep the red spheres from the walls, that they would soon be overwhelming us.

'It does not matter,' she piped. 'The Eternal Ones have found us again.'

Looking nervously about, I saw the bars of ghostly light once more. Seven thin upright pillars of silvery radiance, standing in a ring about us. They had exactly the same appearance as those from which we had fled at the pool.

'I have felt them watching for some time,' she said. 'Before, we escaped by running away. Now that is impossible.'

Calmly she coiled her tawny length. The white mantles were folded against her golden fur. Her small head sank upon her coils, blue crest erect above it. Her violet eyes were grave, calm, alert. They reflected neither fear nor despair.

The seven pillars of light about us became continually brighter.

One of the red spheres, with black tentacles extended, dragged itself upon the top of the butte, with us. The Mother saw it, but paid it no heed. It was outside the ring formed by the seven pillars. I stood still, within that ring, beside the Mother, watching – waiting.

The seven columns of light grew brighter.

Then it seemed that they were no longer light, but solid metal. At the same instant, I was blinded with a flash of light, intolerably bright. A splintering crash of sound smote my ears, sharp as the crack of a rifle, infinitely louder. A wave of pain flashed over my body, as if I had received a severe electric shock. I had a sense of abrupt movement, as if the rock beneath my feet had been jarred by a moonquake.

Then we were no longer upon the rock.

I was standing upon a broad, smooth metal plate. About its edge rose seven metal rods, shining with a white light, their positions corresponding exactly to the seven ghostly pillars. The Mother was coiled on the metal plate beside me, her violet eyes still cool and quiet, revealing no surprise.

But I was dazed with astonishment.

For we were no longer in the jungle. The metal plate upon which I stood was part of a complex mechanism, of bars and coils of shining wire, and huge tubes of transparent crystal, which stood in the centre of a broad open court, paved with bright, worn metal.

About the court towered buildings. Lofty, rectangular edifices of metal and transparent crystal. They were not beautiful structures. Nor were they in good repair. The metal was covered with ugly red oxide. Many of the crystal panels were shattered.

Along the metal-paved streets, and on the wide courtyards about us, things were moving. Not human beings. Not evidently, living things at all. But grotesque things of metal. Machines. They had no common standard of form; few seemed to resemble any others. They had apparently been designed with a variety of shapes, to fill a variety of purposes.

But many had a semblance to living things that was horrible mockery.

'This is the land of the Eternal Ones,' the Mother piped to me softly. 'These are the beings that destroyed my people, seeking new brains for their worn-out machines.'

'But how did we get here?' I demanded.

'Evidently they have developed means of transmitting matter through space. A mere technical question. Resolving matter into energy, transmitting the energy without loss on a light beam, condensing it again into the original atoms.

'It is not remarkable that the Eternal Ones can do such things. When they gave up all that is life, for such power. When they sacrificed their bodies for machines. Should they not have some reward?

'It seems impossible –'

'It must, to you. The science of your world is young. If you have television after a few hundred years, what will you not have developed after a hundred thousand?

'Even to the Eternal Ones, it is new. It is only in the time of my own life that they have been able to transmit objects between two stations, without destroying their identity. And they have never before used this apparatus, with carrier rays that could reach out to disintegrate our bodies upon the rock, and create a reflecting zone of interference that would focus the beam here –'

Her piping notes broke off sharply. Three grotesque machines were advancing upon us, about the platform. Queer bright cases, with levels and wheels projecting from them. Jointed metal limbs. Upon the top of each was a transparent crystal dome, containing a strange, shapeless grey mass. A soft helpless grey thing, with huge black staring eyes. The brain in the machine! The Eternal One.

Horrible travesties of life, were those metal things. At first they appeared almost alive, with their quick, sure movements. But mechanical sounds came from them, little clatterings and hummings. They were stark and ugly.

And their eyes roughened my skin with dread. Huge, black, and cold. There was nothing warm in them, nothing human, nothing kind. They were as emotionless as polished lenses. And filled with menace.

'They shall not take me alive!' the Mother piped, lifting herself beside me on tawny coils.

Then, as if something had snapped like a taut wire in my mind, I ran at the nearest of the Eternal Ones, my eyes searching swiftly for a weapon.

It was one of the upright metal rods that I seized. Its lower end was set in an oddly shaped mass of white crystal, which I took to be an insulator of some kind. It shattered when I threw my weight on the rod. And the rod came free in my hands, the white glow vanishing from it, so I saw it was copper.

Thus I was provided with a massive metal club, as heavy as I could readily swing. On earth, it would have weighed far more than I could lift.

Raising it over my head, I sprang in front of the foremost of the advancing machines – a case of bright metal, moving stiffly upon metal limbs, with a dome-shaped shell of crystal upon it, which housed the helpless grey brain, with its black, unpleasant eyes. I saw little tentacles – feeble translucent fingers – reaching from the brain to touch controlling levers.

The machine paused before me. An angry, insistent buzzing came from it. A great, hooked, many-jointed metal lever reached out from it suddenly, as if to seize me.

And I struck, bringing the copper bar down upon the transparent dome with all my strength. The crystal was tough. But the inertia of the copper bar was as great as it would have been upon the earth; its hundreds of pounds came down with a force indeed terrific.

The dome was shattered. And the grey brain smashed into red pulp.

The Eternal Ones would certainly have been able to seize the Mother, without suffering any harm. And probably any other creature of the moon, that might have been brought with her on the matter-transmitting beam. But they were not equipped for dealing with a being whose muscles were the stronger ones of earth.

The two fellows of the Eternal One I had destroyed fell upon me. Though the copper bar was not very heavy, it was oddly hard to swing, because of its great inertia. The metal limbs of the third machine closed about my body, even as I crushed the brain in the second with another smashing blow.

I squirmed desperately, but I was unable to twist about to get in a position to strike.

Then the Mother was gliding toward me. Blue crest erect upon her golden head, eager light of battle flashing in her violet eyes. From her smooth, tawny sides the mantles were stiffly outstretched. And they were almost scarlet with the flashing lights that played through them. My momentary despair vanished; I felt that she was invincible.

She almost reached me. And then rose upon her glossy coils, and gazed at the brain in the transparent dome of the machine that held me, her membranes still alight.

Abruptly the machine released me; its metal limbs were relaxed, motionless.

My encrimsoned copper mace rose and descended once more, and the machine fell with a clatter upon its side.

'My mental energy is greater than that of the Eternal One,' the Mother piped in calm explanation. 'I was able to interfere with its neural processes to cause paralysis.' She looked about us suddenly.

'But smash the delicate parts of this machine that brought us here. So that if we have the good fortune to escape, they cannot soon bring us back. I know it is the only one they have, and it does not look as if it could be quickly repaired.'

My club was busy again. Delicate coils were battered beneath it. Complex prisms and mirrors and lenses shattered. Delicate wires and grids in crystal shells, which must have been electron tubes, destroyed.

The three machines we had wrecked had been the only ones near. But a score or more of others were soon approaching across the metal-paved court, producing buzzing sounds as if of anger and excitement. Some of them were near before my work was done.

Too many of them to battle. We must attempt an escape.

I stooped, picked up the Mother's warm, downy body, and ran across the platform. toward the ring of approaching machine beings. Near them, I leaped, as high and as far as I could.

The spring carried me over them, and a good many yards beyond. In a moment I was in the middle of a worn pavement of metal. The street, almost empty of the machines, ran between ancient and ugly buildings, toward a lofty wall of some material black and brilliant as obsidian.

I hastened desperately toward the wall, moving with great

leaps. The Eternal Ones followed in humming, clattering confusion, falling swiftly behind.

They had been taken quite by surprise, of course. And, as the Mother had said, dependence upon the machine had not developed in them the ability to respond quickly to emergencies.

As we later discovered, some of the machines could travel much faster than we could. But, as I have remarked, the things were not of a standard design, all differing. And none of those behind us happened to be of the fastest type.

I do not doubt that they could easily have destroyed us, as we fled. But their object would have been defeated. They wanted the Mother alive.

We reached the shining black wall well ahead of our pursuers. Its surface was smooth and perpendicular; it was fully as high as the cliff up which I had leaped with the Mother. And there was no projecting ledge to save us if I fell short.

I paused, dropping the heavy mace.

'You could toss me up,' the Mother suggested. 'Then leap.'

There was no time for delay. She coiled quickly up into a golden sphere. I hurled her upward, like a football. She vanished over the top of the wall. I lifted the mace, threw it up, and to one side, so it would not strike her.

The Eternal Ones were close behind. A mob-like group of grotesque machines. Buzzing angrily. One of them flung some missile. There was a crashing explosion against the black wall, a flare of green light. I realized the danger of being separated from the Mother, even as I leaped.

My spring carried me completely over the wall, which was only some five or six feet thick.

I descended into a luxuriant tangle of the green creepers. Foot-thick stems covered the ground in an unbroken network, feathery leaves rising from them higher than my head. I fell on my side in the delicate foliage, struggled quickly to my feet. The green fronds cut off my view in all directions, though I could see the top of the black wall above.

Before I struck the ground I had glimpsed a vast green plain lying away eastward to the horizon. In the north was a distant line of red mountains. The city of the Eternal Ones lay westward.

I saw nothing of the Mother; I could not, in truth, see a dozen feet through the exotic jungle.

'This way,' her cautious whistling tones reached me in a moment. 'Here is your weapon.'

I broke through the masses of delicate fronds in the direction of the sound, found the Mother unharmed, coiled in a golden circle beside the copper bar. She glided silently away; I picked up the bar and followed as rapidly and quietly as I could.

Once I looked back, when we passed a narrow open space, and saw a little group of the Eternal Ones standing upon the black wall. They must have been looking after us, but I do not suppose they saw us.

For the rest of the day – it was early afternoon when we escaped – and all night when the jungle was weird and silvery in the earth light, and until late on the following day, we hastened on. We did not stop except to drink and bathe at a little stream, and to scrape the sweet white powder from a few of the great argent flowers we passed. We ate as we moved. The jungle of creepers was unbroken; we were always hidden in the luxuriant, delicate foliage.

At first I had been sure we would be followed. But as the hours passed and there was no sign of pursuit, my spirits rose. I doubted now that the Eternal Ones could follow the trail swiftly enough to overtake us. But I still carried the copper mace.

The Mother was less optimistic than I.

'I know they are following,' she told me. 'I feel them. But we may lose them. If they cannot repair the machine which you wrecked – and I am sure they cannot do it soon.'

We had approached a rocky slope, and the Mother found a little cave, beneath an overhanging ledge, in which we rested. Totally exhausted, I threw myself down, and slept like a dead man.

It was early on the next morning when the Mother woke me. She lay coiled at the entrance of the cave, the frail mantles stiffened and flushed a little with rosy light, violet eyes grave and watchful.

'The Eternal Ones follow,' she piped. 'They are yet far off. But we must go on.'

VIII

AN EARTHMAN FIGHTS

Climbing to the top of the rocky slope, we came out upon a vast plateau, covered with green moss. The level surface was broken here and there by low hills; but no other vegetation was in view before us. At a distance, the plain resembled a weird desert covered with green snow.

It took six days to cross the moss-grown table land. We finished the white powder we had carried with us on the fourth day; and we found no water on the fifth or sixth. Though, of course, those days were of only eighteen hours each, we were in a sorry plight when we descended into a valley green with the creepers, watered with a crystal stream whose water seemed the sweetest I had ever tasted.

We ate and rested for two nights and a day, before we went on – though the Mother insisted that the Eternal Ones still followed.

Then, for seventeen days, we followed down the stream, which was joined by countless tributaries until it became a majestic river. On the seventeenth day, the river flowed into a still greater one, which came down a valley many miles wide, covered with yellow thorn brush and green creepers, and infested with thousands of the purple balloon creatures, which I had learned to avoid by keeping to the green jungle, where they could not throw their webs with accuracy.

We swam the river, and continued down the eastern bank – it was flowing generally south. Five days later we came in view of a triple peak I well remembered.

Next morning we left the jungle, and climbed up to the little moss-carpeted plateau where I had left the machine. I had feared that it somehow would be gone, or wrecked. But it lay just as I had left it on the day after I landed on the moon. Bright, polished, window-studded wall of armour, between two projecting plates of gleaming copper.

We reached the door, the Mother gliding beside me.

Trembling with a great eagerness, I turned the knob and opened it. Everything was in order, just as I had left it. The oxygen cylinders, the batteries, the food refrigerator, the central control table, with the chart lying upon it.

In a week – if the mechanism worked as I hoped it would – I should be back upon the earth. Back on Long Island. Ready to report to my uncle, and collect the first payment of my fifty thousand a year.

Still standing on the narrow deck outside the door, I looked down at the Mother.

She was coiled at my feet. The blue plume upon her golden head seemed to droop. The white mantles were limp, dragging. Her violet eyes, staring up at me, somehow seemed wistful and sad.

Abruptly an ache sprang into my heart, and my eyes dimmed, so that the bright golden image of her swam before me. I had hardly realized what her companionship had come to mean to me, in our long days together. Strange as her body was, the Mother had come to be almost human in my thoughts. Loyal, courageous, kind – a comrade.

'You must go with me,' I stammered, in a voice gone oddly husky. 'Don't know whether the machine will ever get back to earth or not. But at least it will carry us out of reach of the Eternal Ones.'

For the first time, the musical pipings of the Mother seemed broken and uneven, as if with emotion.

'No. We have been together long, Adventurer. And parting is not easy. But I have a great work. The seed of my kind is in me, and it must not die. The Eternal Ones are near. But I will not give up the battle until I am dead.'

Abruptly she lifted her tawny length beside me. The limp, pallid mantles were suddenly bright and strong again. They seized my hands in a grasp convulsively tight. The Mother gazed up at my face, for a little time, with deep violet eyes – earnest and lonely and wistful, with the tragedy of her race in them.

Then she dropped and glided swiftly away.

I looked after her with misty eyes, until she was half across the plateau. On her way to the sea, to find a home for the new race she was to rear. With leaden heart, and an aching constriction in my throat, I climbed through the oval door, into the machine, and fastened it.

But I did not approach the control table. I stood at the little round windows, watching the Mother gliding away, across the carpet of moss. Going ahead alone . . . the last of her race. . . .

Then I looked in the other direction, and saw the Eternal

Ones. She had said the machines were near. I saw five of them. They were moving swiftly across the plateau, the way we had come.

Five grotesque machines. Their bright metal cases were larger than those of the ones we had encountered in the city. And their limbs were longer. They stalked like moving towers of metal, each upon four jointed stilts. And long, flail-like limbs dangled from the case of each. Crystal domes crowned them, sparkling in the sunlight – covering, I knew, the feeble grey brains that controlled them. The Eternal Ones.

Almost at the edge of the plateau they were when I first saw them. I had time easily to finish sealing the door, to close the valve through which I had let out the excess air upon landing, and to drive up through the moon's atmosphere, toward the white planet.

But I did not move to do those things. I stood at the window watching, hands clenched so that nails cut into my palms, set teeth biting through my lip.

Then, as they came on, I moved suddenly, governed not by reason but by an impulse that I could not resist. I opened the door and clambered out, picking up the great copper mace that I had left lying outside.

And I crouched beside the machine, waiting.

Looking across the way the Mother had gone, I saw her at the edge of the plateau. A tiny, distant form, upon the green moss. I think she had already seen the machines, and realizing the futility of flight had turned back to face them.

As the machine things came by, I was appalled at their size. The metal stilts were fully six feet long, the vulnerable crystal domes eight feet above the ground.

I leaped up, and struck at the brain of the nearest, as it passed. My blow crushed the transparent shell and the soft brain within it. But the machine toppled toward me, and I fell with it to the ground, cruelly bruised beneath its angular levers.

One leg was fast beneath it, pinned against the ground, and its weight was so great that I could not immediately extricate myself. But I had clung to the copper bar, and when another machine bent down, as if to examine the fallen one, I seized the weapon with both hands, and placed another fatal blow.

The second machine fell stiffly beside me, and odd humming sound continuing within it, in such a position that it almost concealed me from the others. I struggled furiously to free my leg, while the other Eternal Ones gathered about, producing curious buzzing sounds.

At last I was free, and on my knees. Always slow in such an unexpected emergency, the machine beings had taken no action, though they continued the buzzing.

One of them sprang toward me as I moved, striking a flailing blow at me with a metal arm. I leaped up at it, avoiding the sweeping blow, and struck its crystal case with the end of the copper bar.

The bar smashed through the crystal dome, and crushed the frail brain thing within it. But the machine still moved. It went leaping away across the plateau, its metal limbs still going through the same motions as before I had killed the ruling brain.

I fell back to the ground, rolling over quickly to avoid its stalking limbs, and struggling to my feet, still holding grimly to the copper bar.

The remaining machine beings rushed upon me, flailing out with metal limbs. Desperately, I leaped into the air, rising ten feet above their glistening cases. I came down upon the case of one, beside the crystal dome that housed its brain. I braced my feet and struck, before it could snatch at me with its hooked levers.

As it fell to the moss, humming, buzzing and threshing about with bright metal limbs, I leaped from it toward the other, holding the bar before me. But I struck only the metal case, without harming it, and fell from it into the moss.

Before I could stir, the thing drove its metal limb down upon my body. It struck my chest with a force that was agonizing . . . crushing. A rocket of fiery pain seemed to burst in my brain. For a moment, I think, I was unconscious.

Then I was coughing up bloody foam.

I lay on the red moss, unable to move, the grim realization that I would die breaking over me in a black wave, that swept away even my pain. The metal limb had been lifted from me.

Then the Mother was beside me. She had come back.

Her warm smooth furry body was pressed against my side. I saw her violet eyes, misty, appealing. She laid the rose-flushed mantles over my side. The pain went suddenly from it. And I felt new strength, so I could get to my feet, though red mist still came from my nostrils, and I felt a hot stream of blood down my side.

The remaining machine monster was bending, reaching for the Mother. I seized the copper mace again, struck a furious blow at the crystal shell that housed its brain. As it crashed down, beating about blindly and madly with its great metal limbs, my new strength went suddenly from me and I fell again, coughing once more.

A flailing limb struck the Mother a terrific blow, flinging her against the moss many yards away. She crept back to me, brokenly, slowly. Her golden fur was stained with crimson. Her mantles were limp and pale. There was agony in her eyes.

She came to where I lay, collapsed against my side. Very low, her musical tones reached my ears and died abruptly with a choking sound. She had tried to tell me something, and could not.

The last of the Eternal Ones that had followed was dead, and presently the machines ceased their humming and buzzing and threshing about upon the moss.

Through the rest of the day we lay there, side by side, both unable to move. And through the strange night, when the huge white disc of the earth bathed us in silvery splendour, and in my delirium I dreamed alternately of my life upon it, and of my adventures upon this weird moon world, with the Mother.

When the argent earth was low, and we were cold and drenched with dew, lying very close together to benefit from each other's warmth, the wild dreams passed. For a few minutes I was coldly sane. I looked back upon a life that had never any great purpose, that had been lived carelessly, and impulsively. And I was not sorry that I had come to the moon.

I remained with the Mother until she stirred no more, and no effort on my part could rouse her to life. With tears in my eyes, I buried her beneath the green moss. Then stumbling to the ship I climbed in. Sealing the door and starting the machinery, I felt the ship lift quickly toward the distant beckoning earth.

NEL BESTSELLERS

T51277	'THE NUMBER OF THE BEAST'	*Robert Heinlein*	£2.25
T50777	STRANGER IN A STRANGE LAND	*Robert Heinlein*	£1.75
T51382	FAIR WARNING	*Simpson & Burger*	£1.75
T52478	CAPTAIN BLOOD	*Michael Blodgett*	£1.75
T50246	THE TOP OF THE HILL	*Irwin Shaw*	£1.95
T49620	RICH MAN, POOR MAN	*Irwin Shaw*	£1.60
T51609	MAYDAY	*Thomas H. Block*	£1.75
T54071	MATCHING PAIR	*George G. Gilman*	£1.50
T45773	CLAIRE RAYNER'S LIFEGUIDE		£2.50
T53709	PUBLIC MURDERS	*Bill Granger*	£1.75
T53679	THE PREGNANT WOMAN'S		
	BEAUTY BOOK	*Gloria Natale*	£1.25
T49817	MEMORIES OF ANOTHER DAY	*Harold Robbins*	£1.95
T50807	79 PARK AVENUE	*Harold Robbins*	£1.75
T50149	THE INHERITORS	*Harold Robbins*	£1.75
T53231	THE DARK	*James Herbert*	£1.50
T43245	THE FOG	*James Herbert*	£1.50
T53296	THE RATS	*James Herbert*	£1.50
T45528	THE STAND	*Stephen King*	£1.75
T50874	CARRIE	*Stephen King*	£1.50
T51722	DUNE	*Frank Herbert*	£1.75
T52575	THE MIXED BLESSING	*Helen Van Slyke*	£1.75
T38602	THE APOCALYPSE	*Jeffrey Konvitz*	95p

NEL P.O. BOX 11, FALMOUTH TR10 9EN, CORNWALL

Postage Charge:
U.K. Customers 45p for the first book plus 20p for the second book and 14p for each additional book ordered to a maximum charge of £1.63.

B.F.P.O. & EIRE Customers 45p for the first book plus 20p for the second book and 14p for the next 7 books; thereafter 8p per book.

Overseas Customers 75p for the first book and 21p per copy for each additional book.

Please send cheque or postal order (no currency).

Name ....

Address ....

....

Title ....

While every effort is made to keep prices steady, it is sometimes necessary to increase prices at short notice. New English Library reserve the right to show on covers and charge new retail prices which may differ from those advertised in the text or elsewhere.(7)